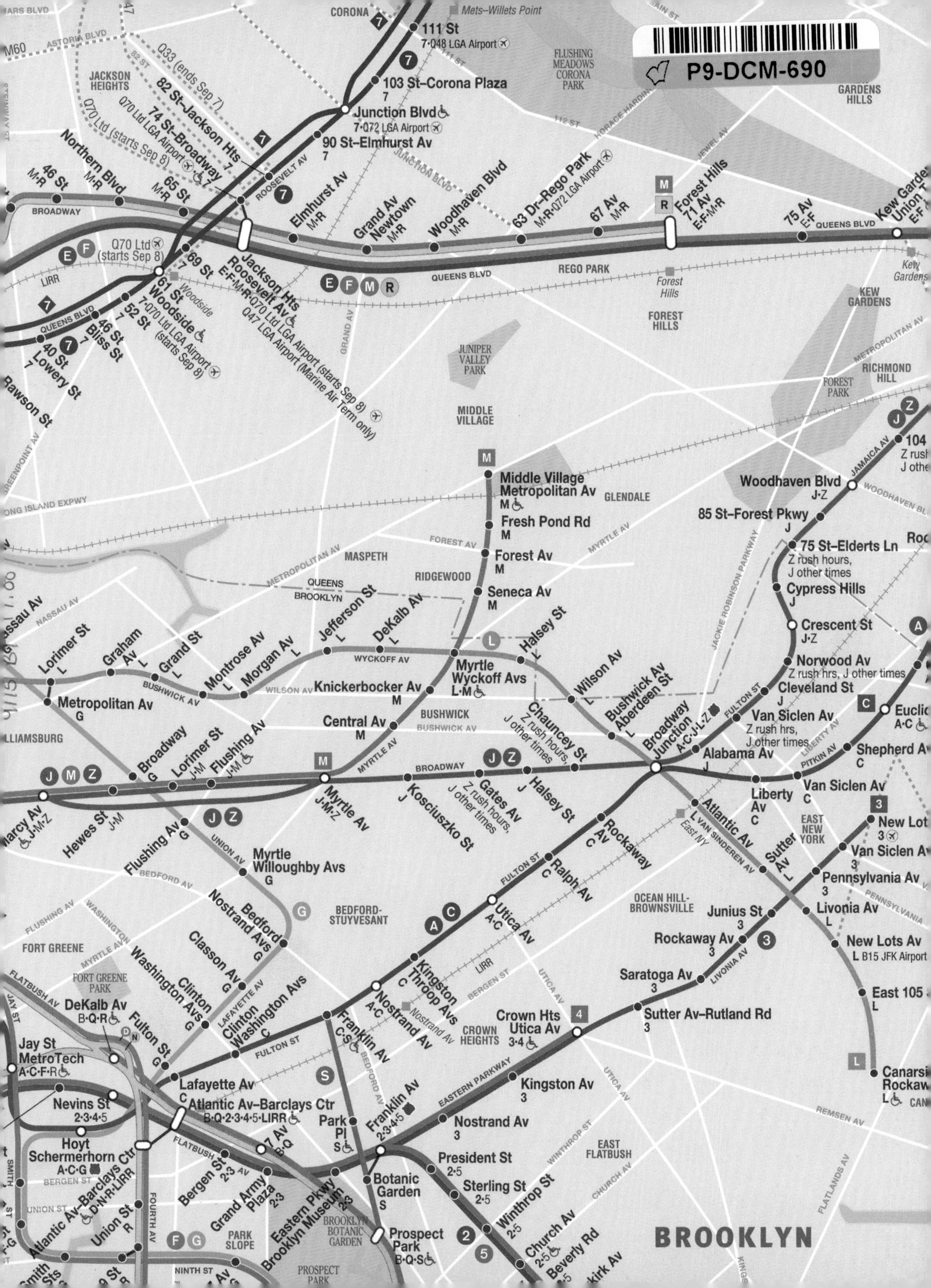
CORONA
Mets–Willets Point
111 St
7·Q48 LGA Airport
103 St–Corona Plaza
7
Junction Blvd
7·Q72 LGA Airport
90 St–Elmhurst Av
7
FLUSHING MEADOWS CORONA PARK
GARDENS HILLS
JACKSON HEIGHTS
ASTORIA BLVD
M60
Q33 (ends Sep 7)
82 St–Jackson Hts
7
74 St–Broadway
Q70 Ltd LGA Airport
Q70 Ltd (starts Sep 8)
Northern Blvd
M·R
46 St
M·R
65 St
M·R
BROADWAY
ROOSEVELT AV
Elmhurst Av
M·R
Grand Av Newtown
M·R
Woodhaven Blvd
M·R
63 Dr–Rego Park
M·R·Q72 LGA Airport
67 Av
M·R
Forest Hills 71 Av
E·F·M·R
75 Av
E·F
QUEENS BLVD
Kew Gardens Union Tpke
E·F
Kew Gardens
Q70 Ltd
(starts Sep 8)
LIRR
69 St
7
Jackson Hts Roosevelt Av
E·F·M·R·Q70 Ltd LGA Airport (starts Sep 8)
Q47 LGA Airport (Marine Air Term only)
61 St Woodside
7·Q70 Ltd LGA Airport (starts Sep 8)
Woodside
52 St
7
46 St Bliss St
7
40 St Lowery St
7
Rawson St
QUEENS BLVD
REGO PARK
Forest Hills
FOREST HILLS
KEW GARDENS
GRAND AV
JUNIPER VALLEY PARK
MIDDLE VILLAGE
METROPOLITAN AV
RICHMOND HILL
FOREST PARK
GREENPOINT AV
LONG ISLAND EXPWY
Middle Village Metropolitan Av
M
Fresh Pond Rd
M
Forest Av
M
Seneca Av
M
GLENDALE
FOREST AV
MYRTLE AV
MASPETH
RIDGEWOOD
QUEENS
BROOKLYN
104 St
Z rush
J other
JAMAICA AV
Woodhaven Blvd
J·Z
WOODHAVEN BL
85 St–Forest Pkwy
J
75 St–Elderts Ln
Z rush hours, J other times
Cypress Hills
J
Crescent St
J·Z
Norwood Av
Z rush hrs, J other times
Cleveland St
J
JACKIE ROBINSON PARKWAY
Nassau Av
NASSAU AV
Lorimer St
L
Graham Av
L
Grand St
L
Montrose Av
L
Morgan Av
L
Jefferson St
L
DeKalb Av
L
WYCKOFF AV
Halsey St
L
Myrtle Wyckoff Avs
L·M
Wilson Av
L
Bushwick Av Aberdeen St
L
Knickerbocker Av
M
WILSON AV
BUSHWICK AV
Metropolitan Av
G
WILLIAMSBURG
Central Av
M
BUSHWICK
Chauncey St
Z rush hours, J other times
Broadway Junction
A·C·J·L·Z
FULTON ST
Van Siclen Av
Z rush hrs, J other times
Euclid Av
A·C
Shepherd Av
C
Alabama Av
J
LIBERTY AV
PITKIN AV
Broadway
G
Lorimer St
J·M
Flushing Av
J·M
Myrtle Av
J·M·Z
MYRTLE AV
BROADWAY
Kosciuszko St
J
Gates Av
Z rush hours, J other times
Halsey St
J
Marcy Av
J·M·Z
Hewes St
J·M
Flushing Av
G
UNION AV
Myrtle Willoughby Avs
G
BEDFORD AV
Rockaway Av
C
Atlantic Av
L
East NY
VAN SINDEREN AV
Liberty Av
C
Van Siclen Av
C
EAST NEW YORK
New Lots Av
3
Van Siclen Av
3
Pennsylvania Av
3
PENNSYLVANIA
Ralph Av
C
Sutter Av
L
Livonia Av
L
Junius St
3
OCEAN HILL-BROWNSVILLE
FLUSHING AV
WASHINGTON
Nostrand Avs
Bedford
G
BEDFORD-STUYVESANT
Utica Av
A·C
Rockaway Av
3
New Lots Av
L B15 JFK Airport
FORT GREENE
MYRTLE AV
FORT GREENE PARK
Classon Av
G
Washington Clinton Avs
G
Kingston Throop Avs
C
LIRR
BERGEN ST
UTICA AV
Saratoga Av
3
LIVONIA AV
East 105 St
L
FLATBUSH AV
DeKalb Av
B·Q·R
Fulton St
G
LAFAYETTE AV
Clinton Washington Avs
C
Nostrand Av
A·C
Nostrand Av
Crown Hts Utica Av
3·4
CROWN HEIGHTS
Sutter Av–Rutland Rd
3
Jay St MetroTech
A·C·F·R
FULTON ST
Franklin Av
C·S
BEDFORD AV
Canarsie Rockaway Pkwy
L
CAN
Lafayette Av
C
Nevins St
2·3·4·5
Atlantic Av–Barclays Ctr
B·Q·2·3·4·5·LIRR
Park Pl
S
Franklin Av
2·3·4·5
EASTERN PARKWAY
Kingston Av
3
Nostrand Av
3
REMSEN AV
UTICA AV
Hoyt Schermerhorn
A·C·G
FLATBUSH AV
7 Av
B·Q
WINTHROP ST
EAST FLATBUSH
President St
2·5
SMITH ST
BERGEN ST
UNION ST
FOURTH AV
Atlantic Av–Barclays Ctr
D·N·R·LIRR
Bergen St
2·3
Grand Army Plaza
2·3
Eastern Pkwy Brooklyn Museum
2·3
Botanic Garden
S
Sterling St
2·5
CHURCH AV
FLATLANDS AV
Union St
R
PARK SLOPE
BROOKLYN BOTANIC GARDEN
Prospect Park
B·Q·S
Winthrop St
2·5
Church Av
2·5
Beverly Rd
BROOKLYN
Smith 9 Sts
9 St
NINTH ST
PROSPECT PARK
Kirk Av

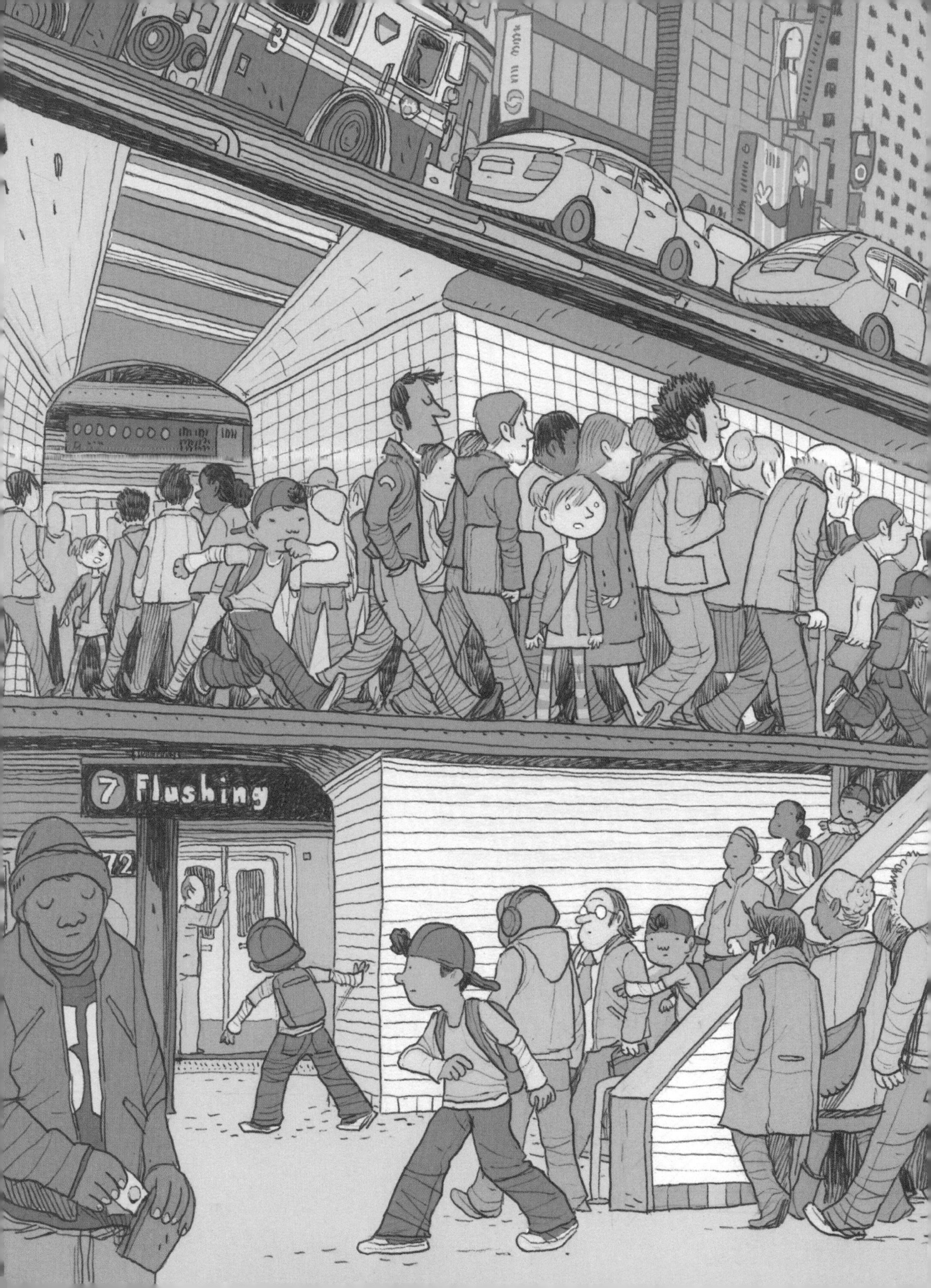
7 Flushing

Lost in
NYC
A SUBWAY ADVENTURE

A TOON GRAPHIC BY

NADJA SPIEGELMAN & SERGIO GARCÍA SÁNCHEZ

For my father, whose answers to my questions made the whole subway car fall silent to listen.
–Nadja

For all those who live without fear of getting lost. And for our children,
the real Pablo and Alicia, who will soon find their way.
–Sergio & Lola

Editorial Director & Book Design: FRANÇOISE MOULY

Deputy Editor & Production: SASHA STEINBERG

Colors: LOLA MORAL

SERGIO GARCÍA SÁNCHEZ'S artwork was drawn in orange pencil
and ballpoint pen and then colored digitally by Lola Moral.

A JUNIOR LIBRARY GUILD SELECTION

FOR VISUAL READERS
TOON
GRAPHICS

OFFICIALLY
LICENSED

A TOON Graphic™ © 2015 Nadja Spiegelman, Sergio García Sánchez & TOON Books, an imprint of RAW Junior, LLC, 27 Greene Street, New York, NY 10013. Subway Map © Metropolitan Transportation Authority. We gratefully acknowledge the help of Arlene Scanlan at Moxie & Co. in obtaining an official license from the MTA for the use of their imagery, symbols and icons. No part of this book may be used or reproduced in any manner whatsoever without written permission except in the case of brief quotations embodied in critical articles and reviews. TOON Graphics™, TOON Books®, LITTLE LIT® and TOON Into Reading!™ are trademarks of RAW Junior, LLC. All rights reserved. All our books are Smyth Sewn (the highest library-quality binding available) and printed with soy-based inks on acid-free, woodfree paper harvested from responsible sources. Printed in Shenzhen, China by Imago. A Spanish edition, *Perdidos en NYC: Una Aventura en el Metro* (ISBN: 978-1-935179-85-6) is also available. Distributed to the trade by Consortium Book Sales and Distribution, Inc.; orders (800) 283-3572; orderentry@perseusbooks.com; www.cbsd.com.
Library of Congress Cataloging-in-Publication Data:
Spiegelman, Nadja.   Lost in NYC : a subway adventure/ by Nadja Spiegelman & Sergio García Sánchez.   pages cm.--   Summary: "After getting separated from his teacher, his classmates, and his trip partner during an outing to the Empire State Building, Pablo, the new kid in school, learns to navigate the New York City subway system as well as his own feelings towards making new friends and living in a big city"--Provided by publisher. ISBN 978-1-935179-81-8   1. Graphic novels. [1. Graphic novels. 2. Subways--Fiction. 3. School field trips--Fiction. 4. Friendship--Fiction. 5. Moving, Household--Fiction. 6. New York (N.Y.)--Fiction.] I. García Sánchez, Sergio, 1967- II. Title.   PZ7.7.S65Lo 2015   741.5'973--dc23   2014028852

ISBN: 978-1-935179-81-8 (hardcover)

15 16 17 18 19 20 IMG 10 9 8 7 6 5 4 3 2 1

WWW.TOON-BOOKS.COM

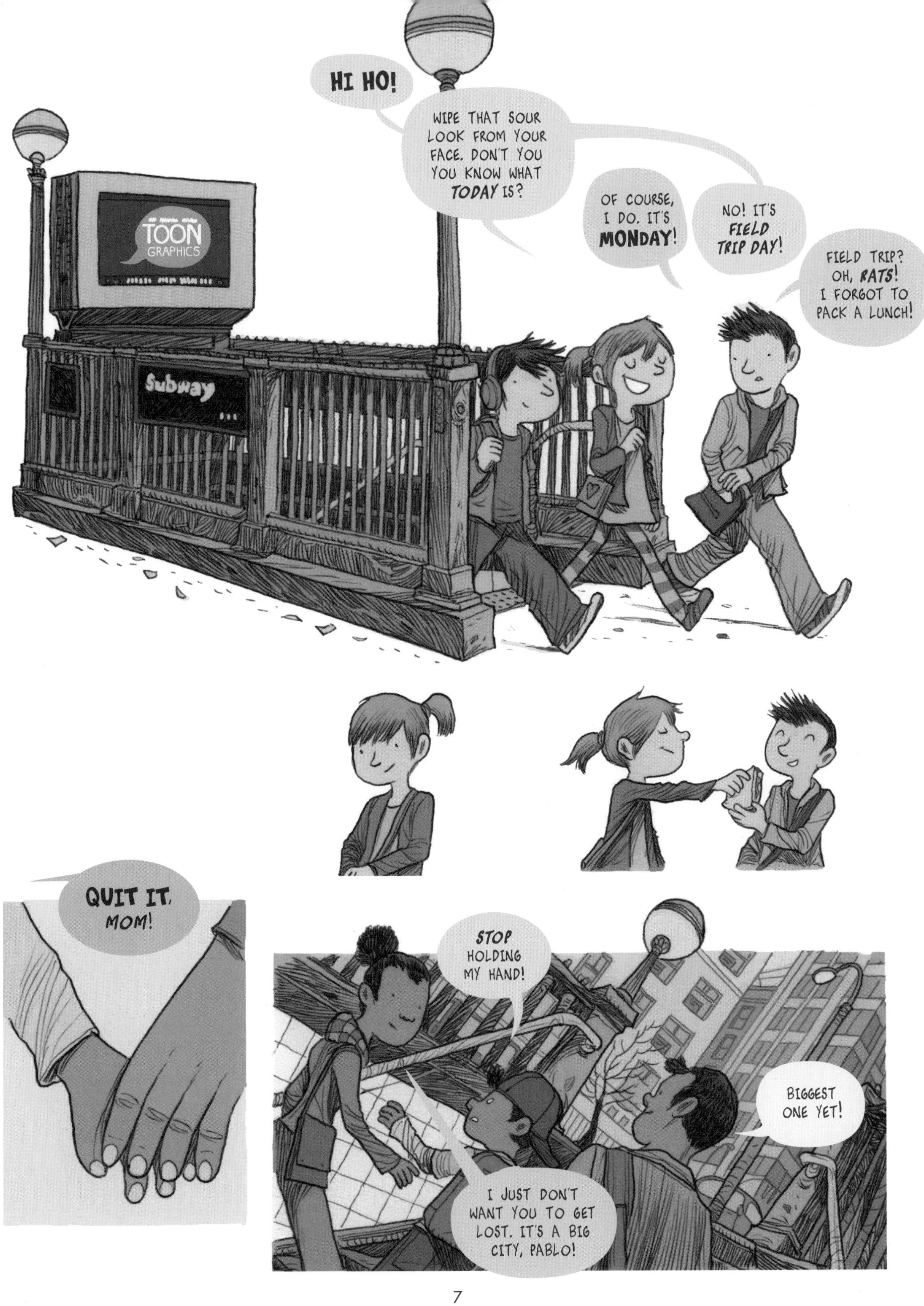
TOON GRAPHICS
Subway
HI HO!
WIPE THAT SOUR LOOK FROM YOUR FACE. DON'T YOU YOU KNOW WHAT **TODAY** IS?
OF COURSE, I DO. IT'S **MONDAY**!
NO! IT'S **FIELD TRIP DAY**!
FIELD TRIP? OH, **RATS**! I FORGOT TO PACK A LUNCH!
QUIT IT, MOM!
STOP HOLDING MY HAND!
I JUST DON'T WANT YOU TO GET LOST. IT'S A BIG CITY, PABLO!
BIGGEST ONE YET!

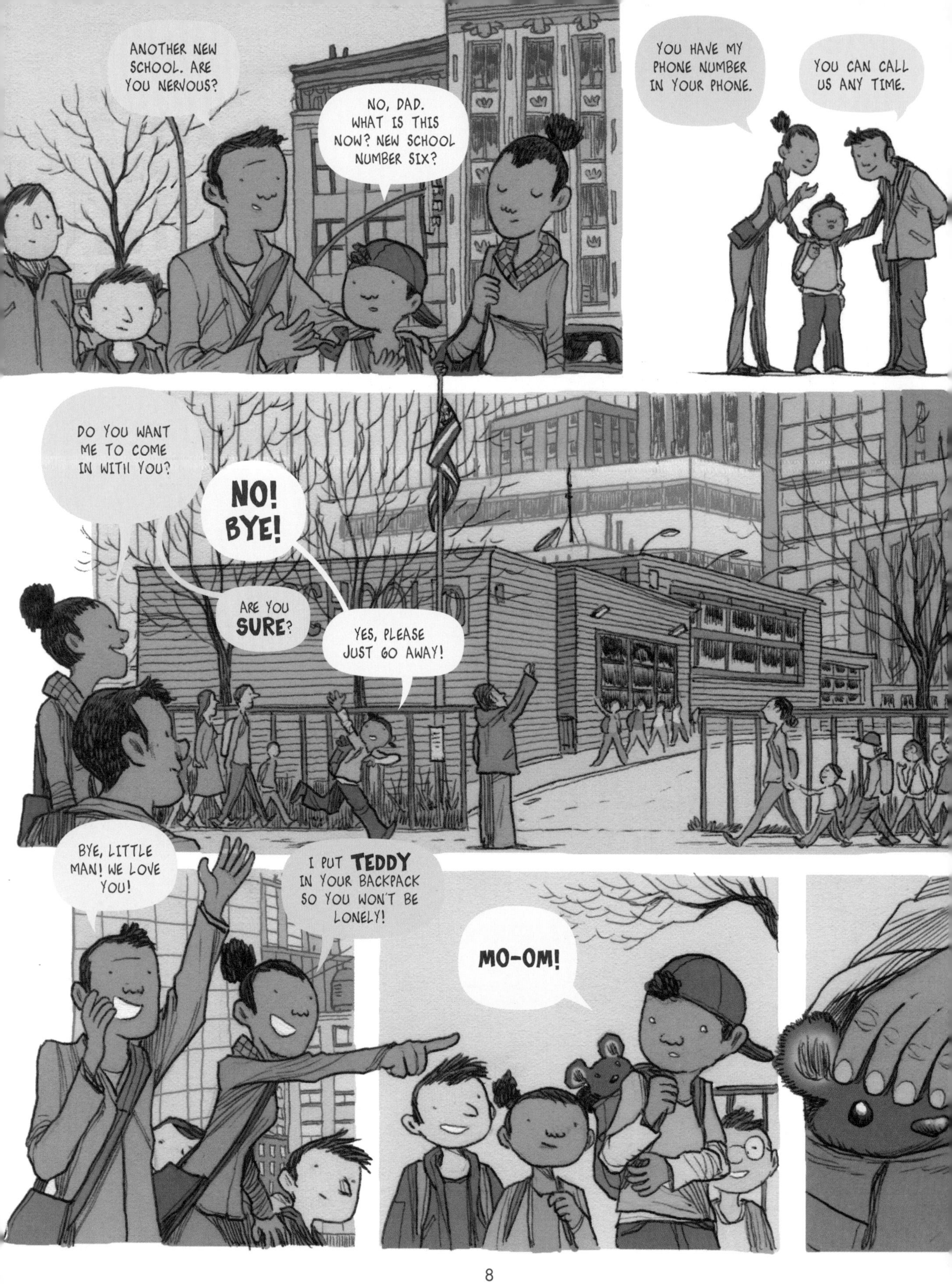
ANOTHER NEW SCHOOL. ARE YOU NERVOUS?
NO, DAD. WHAT IS THIS NOW? NEW SCHOOL NUMBER SIX?
YOU HAVE MY PHONE NUMBER IN YOUR PHONE.
YOU CAN CALL US ANY TIME.
DO YOU WANT ME TO COME IN WITH YOU?
NO! BYE!
ARE YOU SURE?
YES, PLEASE JUST GO AWAY!
BYE, LITTLE MAN! WE LOVE YOU!
I PUT TEDDY IN YOUR BACKPACK SO YOU WON'T BE LONELY!
MO-OM!

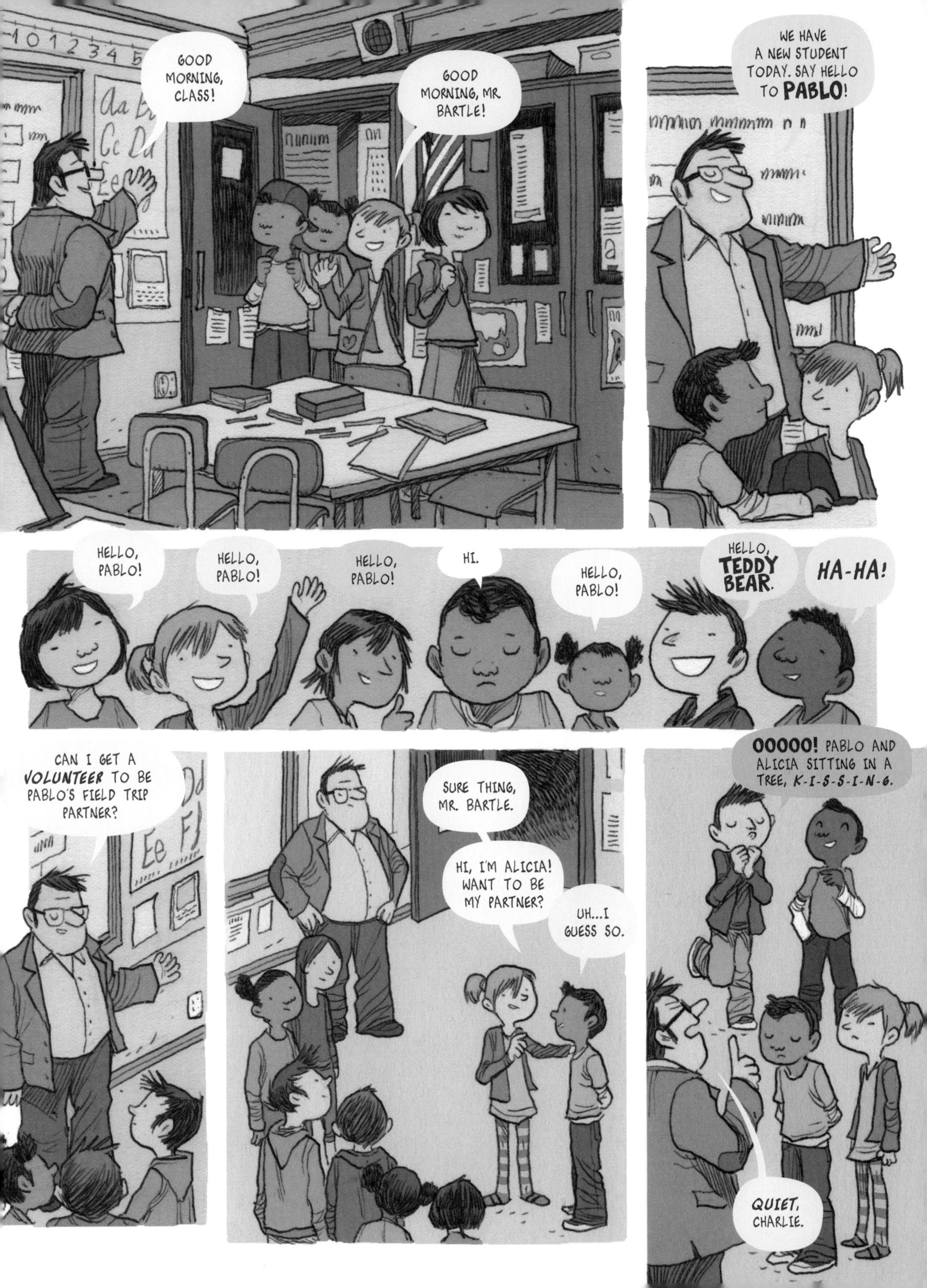
GOOD MORNING, CLASS!
GOOD MORNING, MR BARTLE!
WE HAVE A NEW STUDENT TODAY. SAY HELLO TO PABLO!
HELLO, PABLO!
HELLO, PABLO!
HELLO, PABLO!
HI.
HELLO, PABLO!
HELLO, TEDDY BEAR.
HA-HA!
CAN I GET A VOLUNTEER TO BE PABLO'S FIELD TRIP PARTNER?
SURE THING, MR. BARTLE.
HI, I'M ALICIA! WANT TO BE MY PARTNER?
UH...I GUESS SO.
OOOOO! PABLO AND ALICIA SITTING IN A TREE, K-I-S-S-I-N-G.
QUIET, CHARLIE.

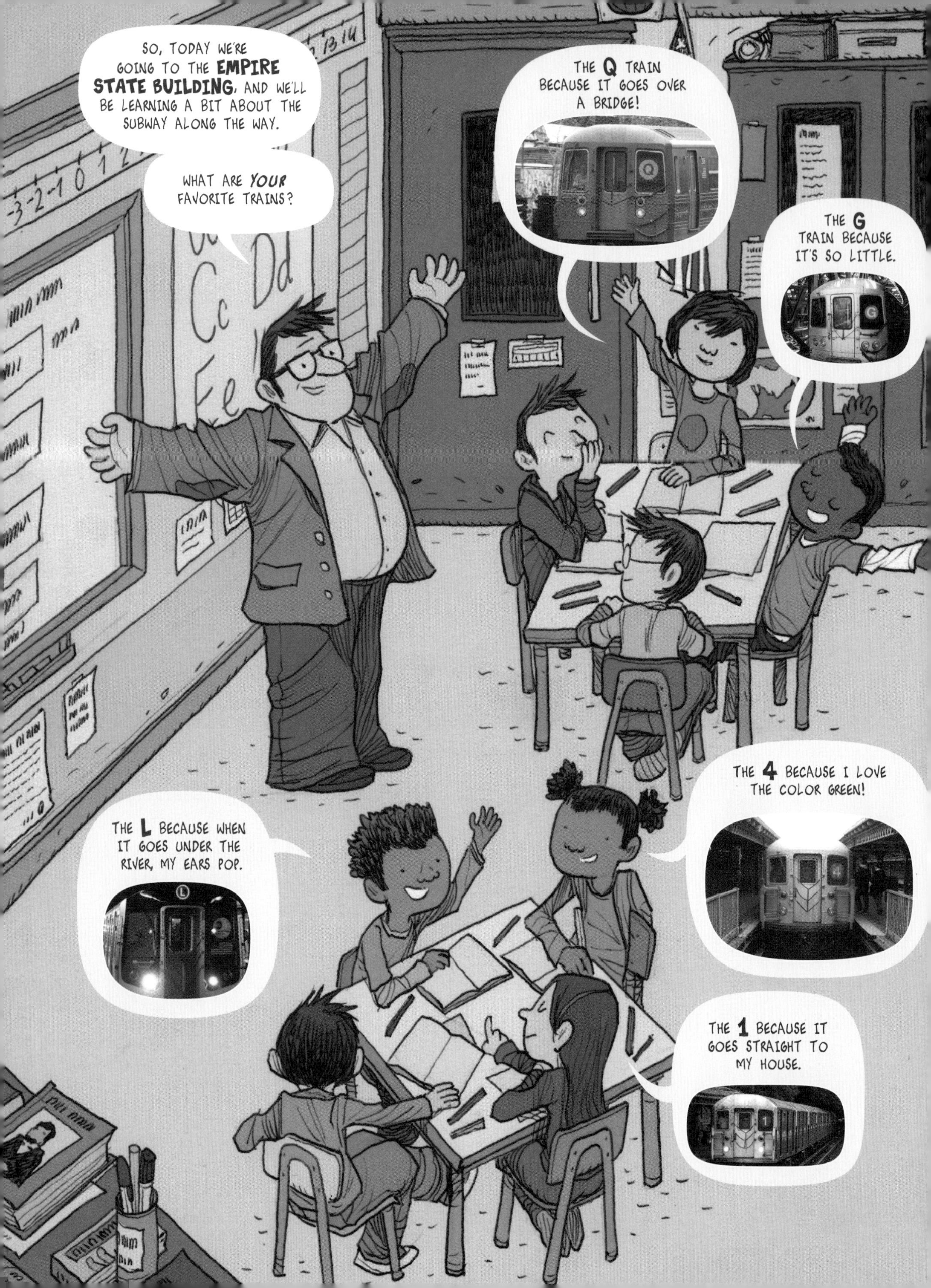
SO, TODAY WE'RE GOING TO THE EMPIRE STATE BUILDING, AND WE'LL BE LEARNING A BIT ABOUT THE SUBWAY ALONG THE WAY.
WHAT ARE YOUR FAVORITE TRAINS?
THE Q TRAIN BECAUSE IT GOES OVER A BRIDGE!
THE G TRAIN BECAUSE IT'S SO LITTLE.
THE 4 BECAUSE I LOVE THE COLOR GREEN!
THE L BECAUSE WHEN IT GOES UNDER THE RIVER, MY EARS POP.
THE 1 BECAUSE IT GOES STRAIGHT TO MY HOUSE.

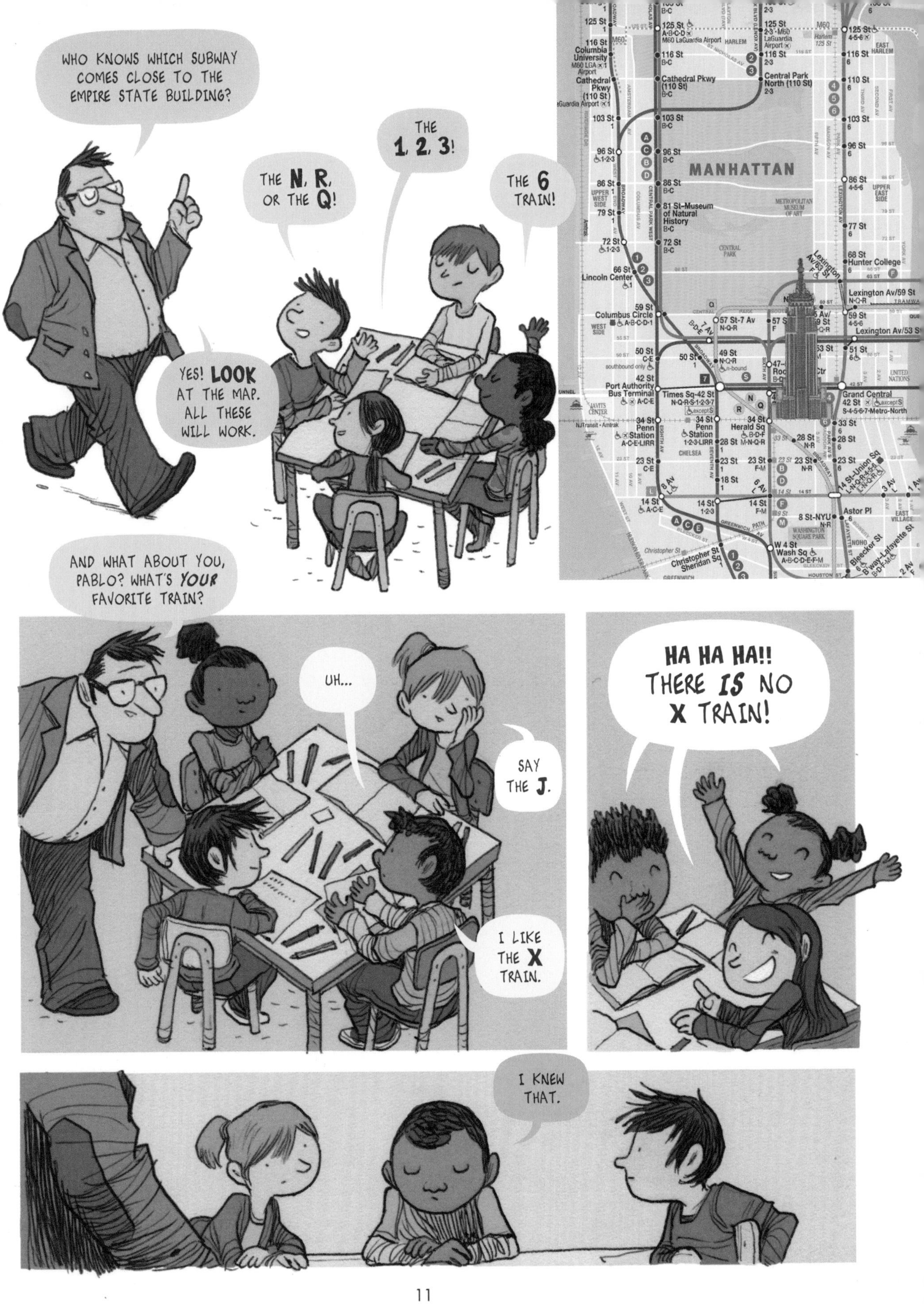
WHO KNOWS WHICH SUBWAY COMES CLOSE TO THE EMPIRE STATE BUILDING?
THE N, R, OR THE Q!
THE 1, 2, 3!
THE 6 TRAIN!
YES! LOOK AT THE MAP. ALL THESE WILL WORK.
MANHATTAN
AND WHAT ABOUT YOU, PABLO? WHAT'S YOUR FAVORITE TRAIN?
UH...
SAY THE J.
I LIKE THE X TRAIN.
HA HA HA!! THERE IS NO X TRAIN!
I KNEW THAT.

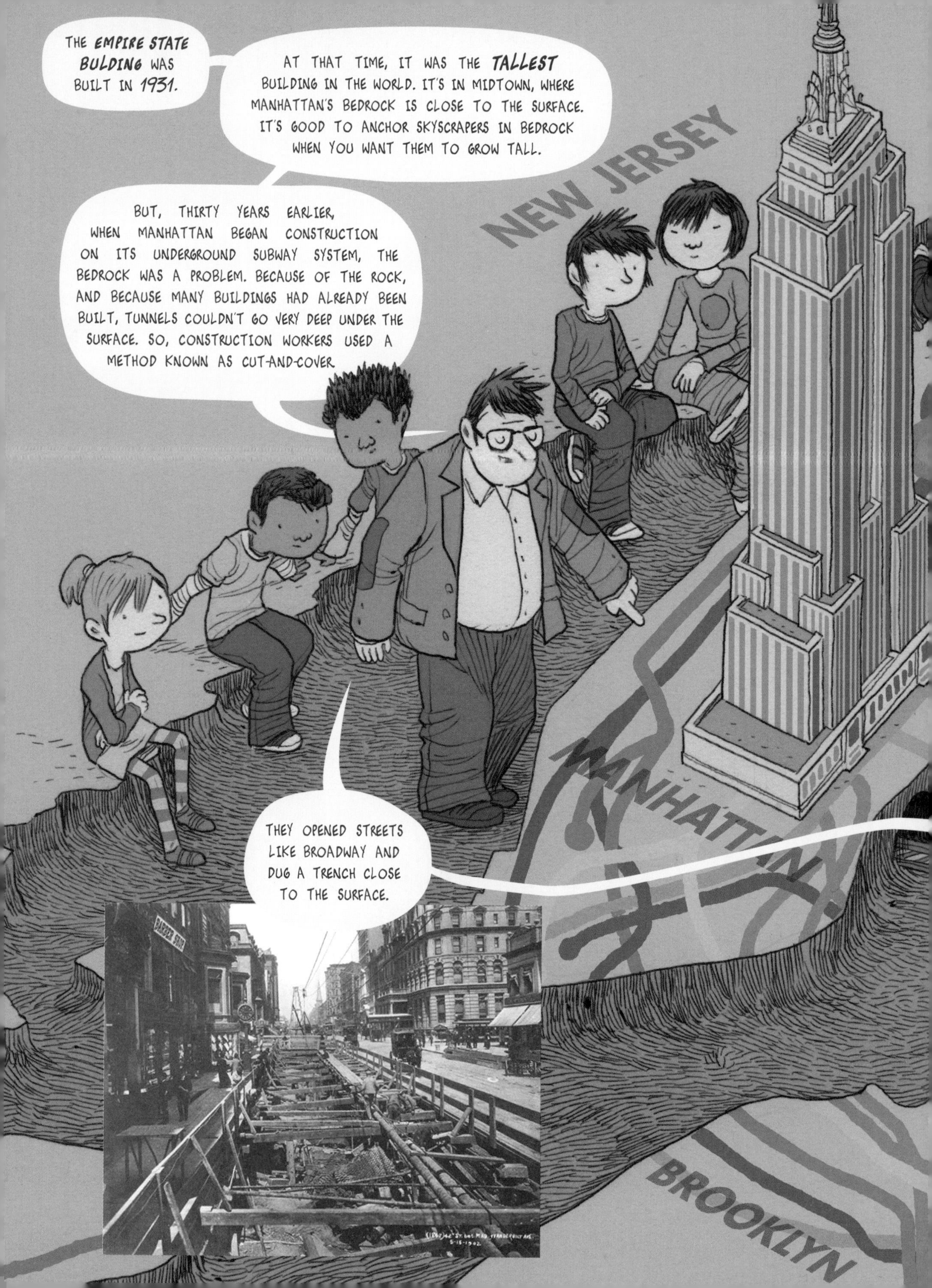
THE EMPIRE STATE BUILDING WAS BUILT IN 1931.
AT THAT TIME, IT WAS THE TALLEST BUILDING IN THE WORLD. IT'S IN MIDTOWN, WHERE MANHATTAN'S BEDROCK IS CLOSE TO THE SURFACE. IT'S GOOD TO ANCHOR SKYSCRAPERS IN BEDROCK WHEN YOU WANT THEM TO GROW TALL.
BUT, THIRTY YEARS EARLIER, WHEN MANHATTAN BEGAN CONSTRUCTION ON ITS UNDERGROUND SUBWAY SYSTEM, THE BEDROCK WAS A PROBLEM. BECAUSE OF THE ROCK, AND BECAUSE MANY BUILDINGS HAD ALREADY BEEN BUILT, TUNNELS COULDN'T GO VERY DEEP UNDER THE SURFACE. SO, CONSTRUCTION WORKERS USED A METHOD KNOWN AS CUT-AND-COVER.
NEW JERSEY
THEY OPENED STREETS LIKE BROADWAY AND DUG A TRENCH CLOSE TO THE SURFACE.
MANHATTAN
BROOKLYN

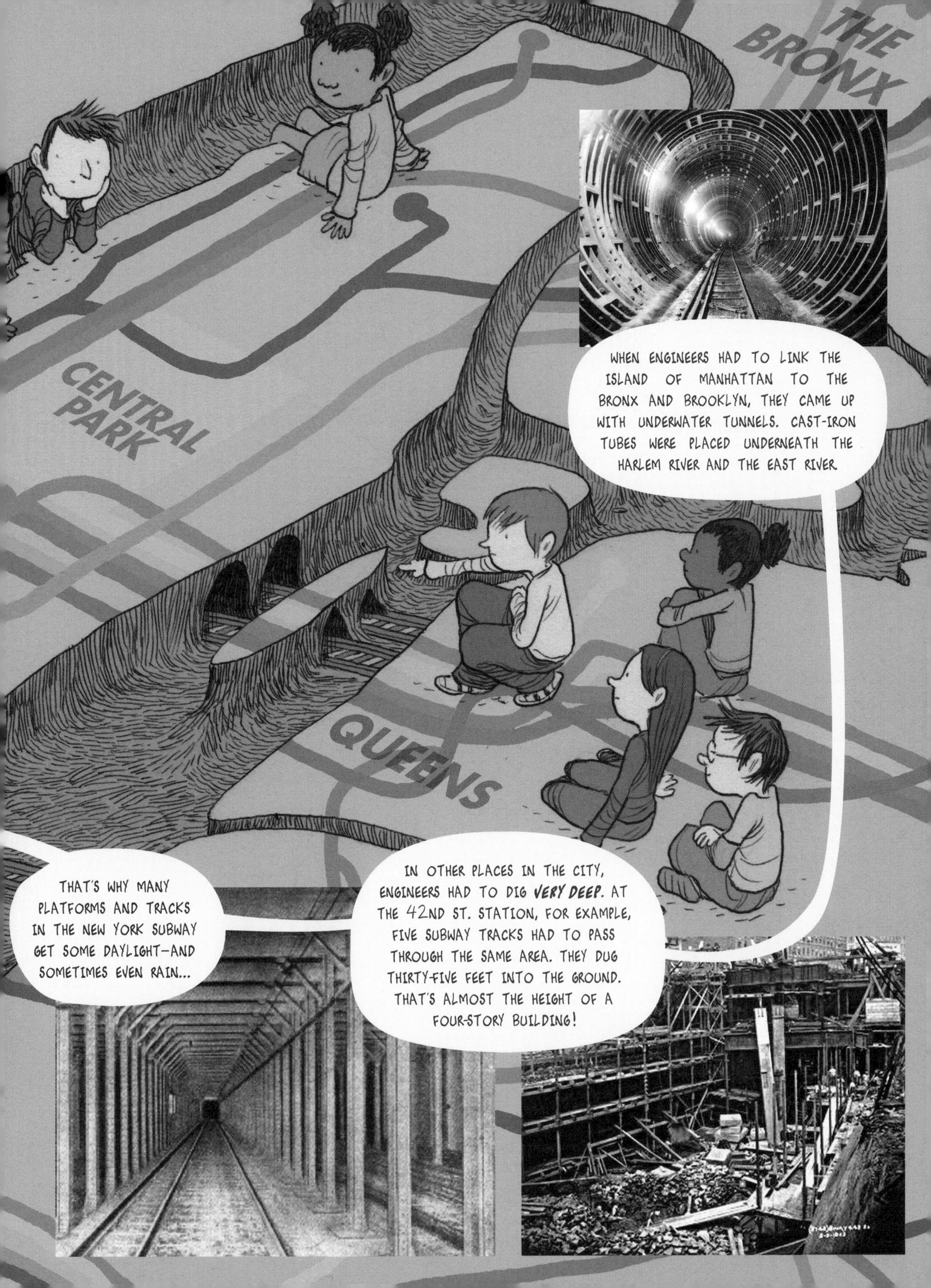

THE BRONX
CENTRAL PARK
QUEENS
THAT'S WHY MANY PLATFORMS AND TRACKS IN THE NEW YORK SUBWAY GET SOME DAYLIGHT—AND SOMETIMES EVEN RAIN...
IN OTHER PLACES IN THE CITY, ENGINEERS HAD TO DIG *VERY DEEP*. AT THE 42ND ST. STATION, FOR EXAMPLE, FIVE SUBWAY TRACKS HAD TO PASS THROUGH THE SAME AREA. THEY DUG THIRTY-FIVE FEET INTO THE GROUND. THAT'S ALMOST THE HEIGHT OF A FOUR-STORY BUILDING!
WHEN ENGINEERS HAD TO LINK THE ISLAND OF MANHATTAN TO THE BRONX AND BROOKLYN, THEY CAME UP WITH UNDERWATER TUNNELS. CAST-IRON TUBES WERE PLACED UNDERNEATH THE HARLEM RIVER AND THE EAST RIVER

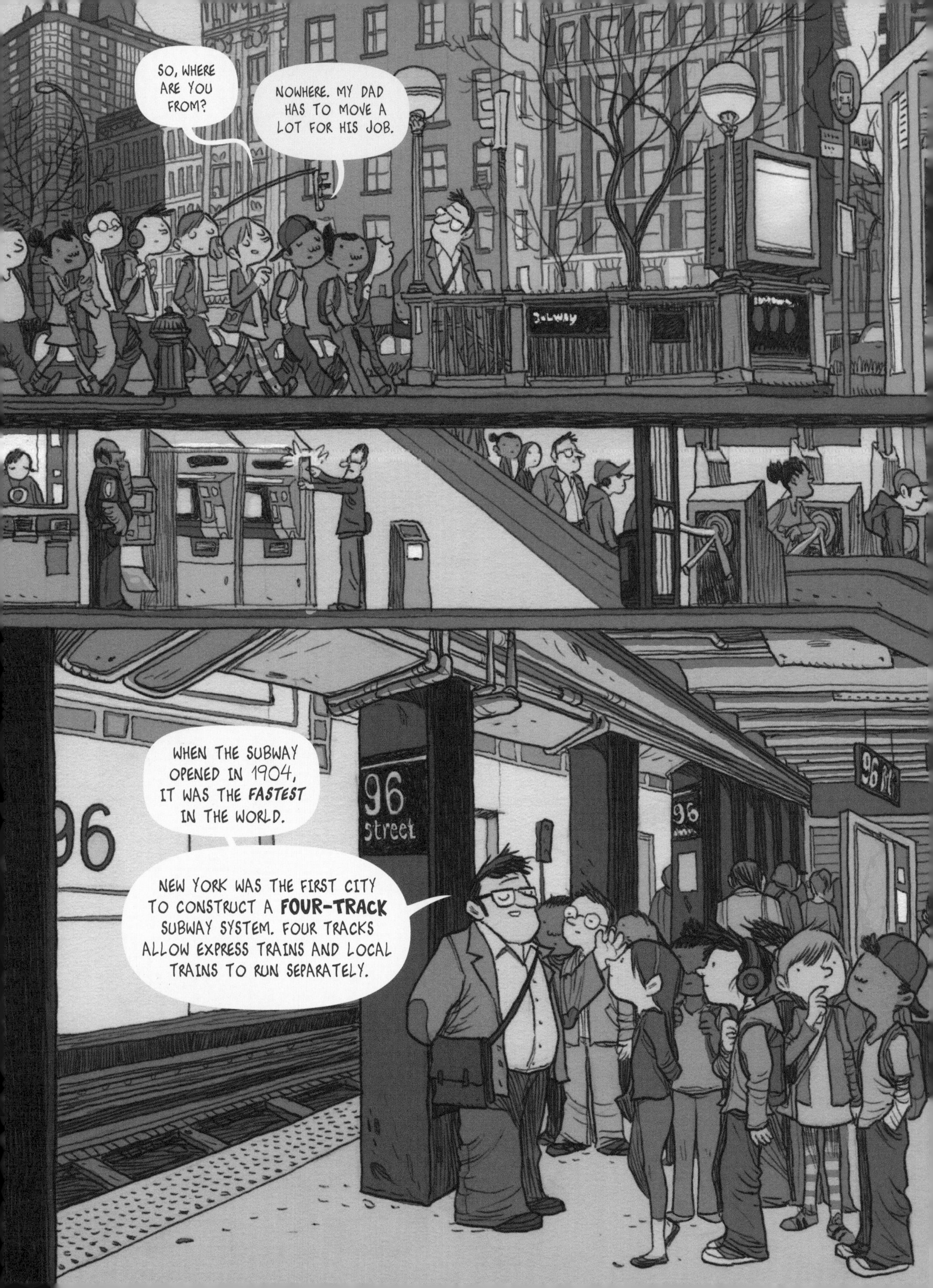
SO, WHERE ARE YOU FROM?
NOWHERE. MY DAD HAS TO MOVE A LOT FOR HIS JOB.
SUBWAY
96 street
96
WHEN THE SUBWAY OPENED IN 1904, IT WAS THE *FASTEST* IN THE WORLD.
NEW YORK WAS THE FIRST CITY TO CONSTRUCT A **FOUR-TRACK** SUBWAY SYSTEM. FOUR TRACKS ALLOW EXPRESS TRAINS AND LOCAL TRAINS TO RUN SEPARATELY.

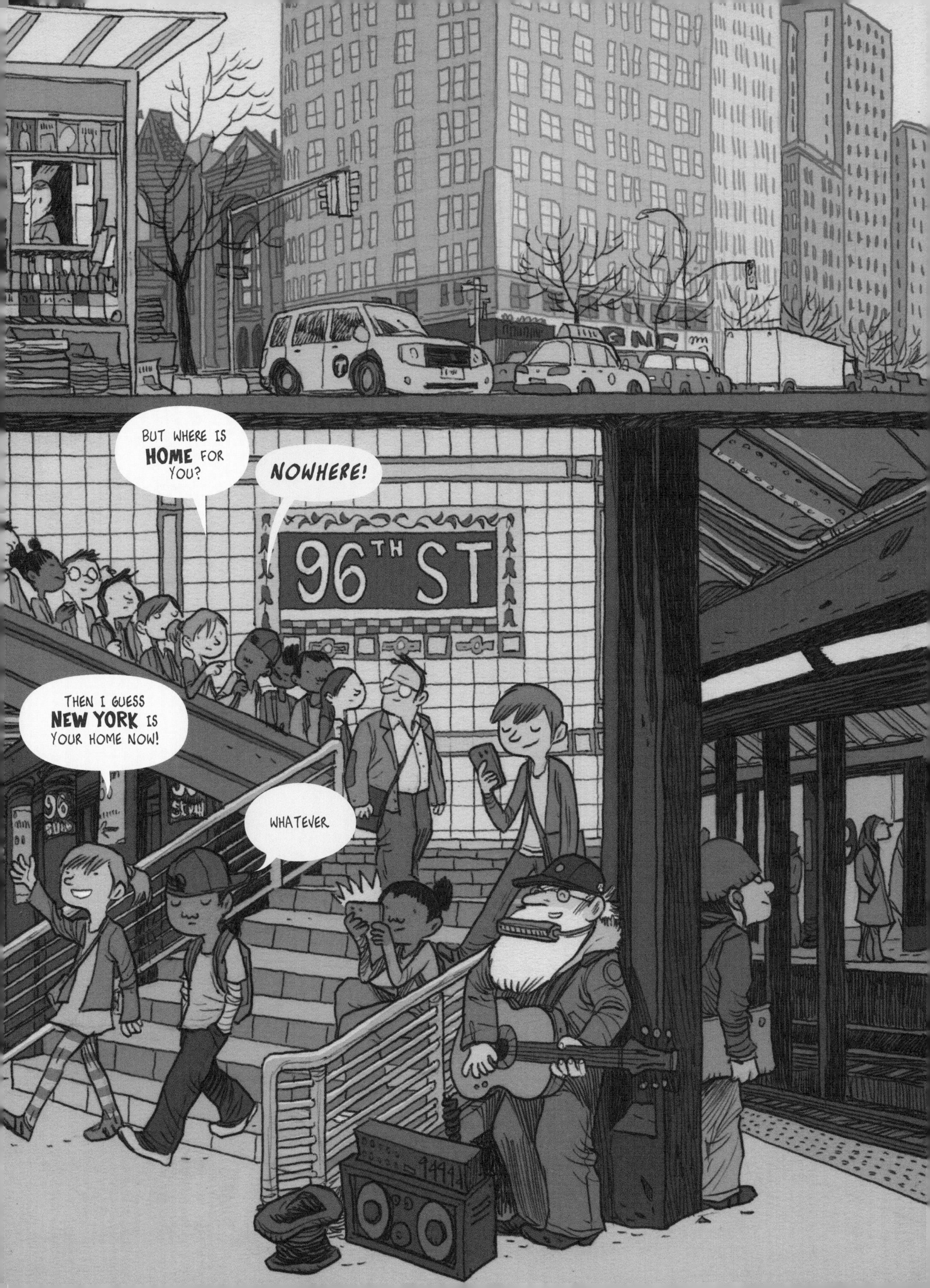

BUT WHERE IS **HOME** FOR YOU?
NOWHERE!
96TH ST
THEN I GUESS **NEW YORK** IS YOUR HOME NOW!
WHATEVER

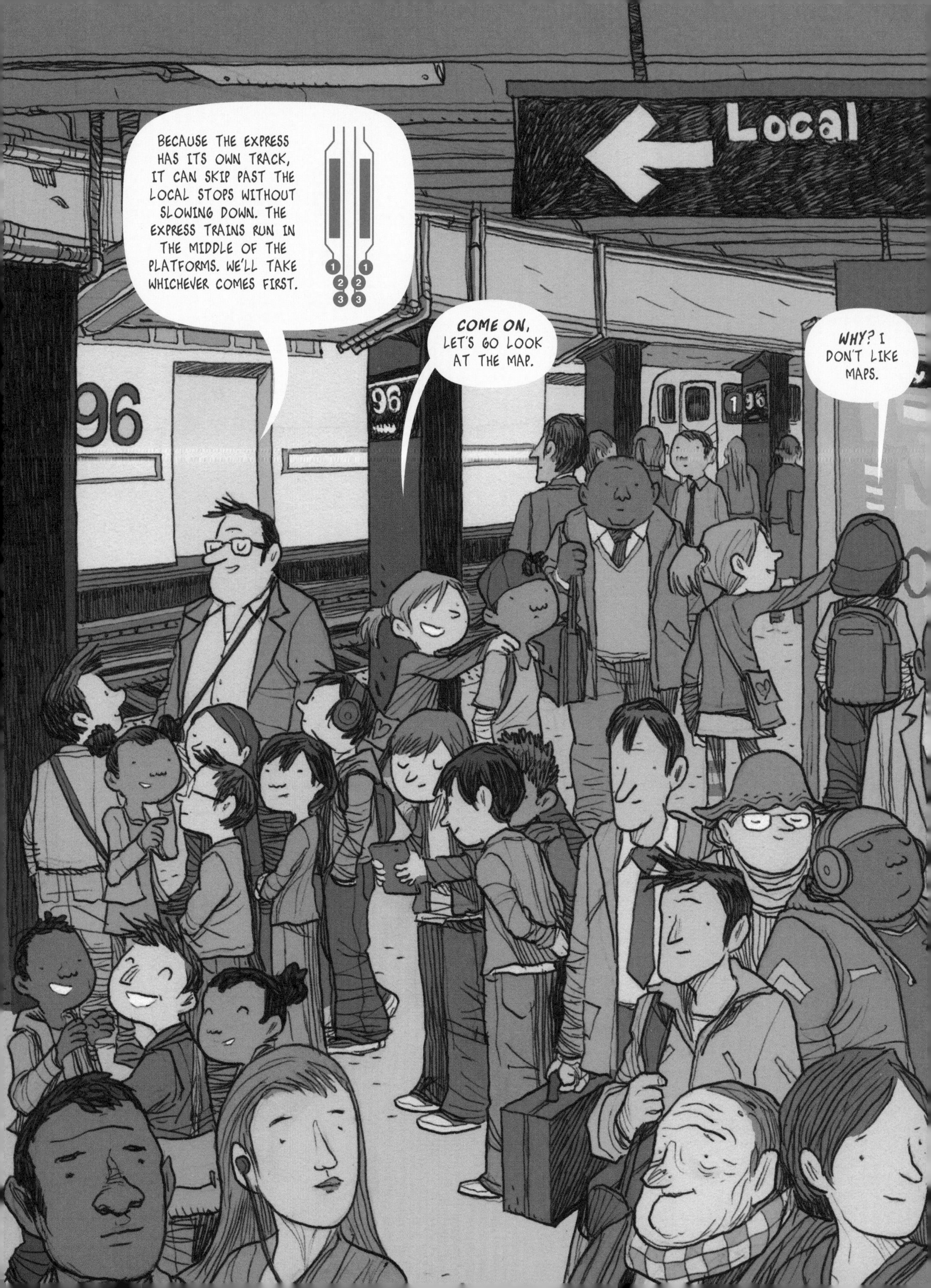
BECAUSE THE EXPRESS HAS ITS OWN TRACK, IT CAN SKIP PAST THE LOCAL STOPS WITHOUT SLOWING DOWN. THE EXPRESS TRAINS RUN IN THE MIDDLE OF THE PLATFORMS. WE'LL TAKE WHICHEVER COMES FIRST.
Local
96
COME ON, LET'S GO LOOK AT THE MAP.
WHY? I DON'T LIKE MAPS.

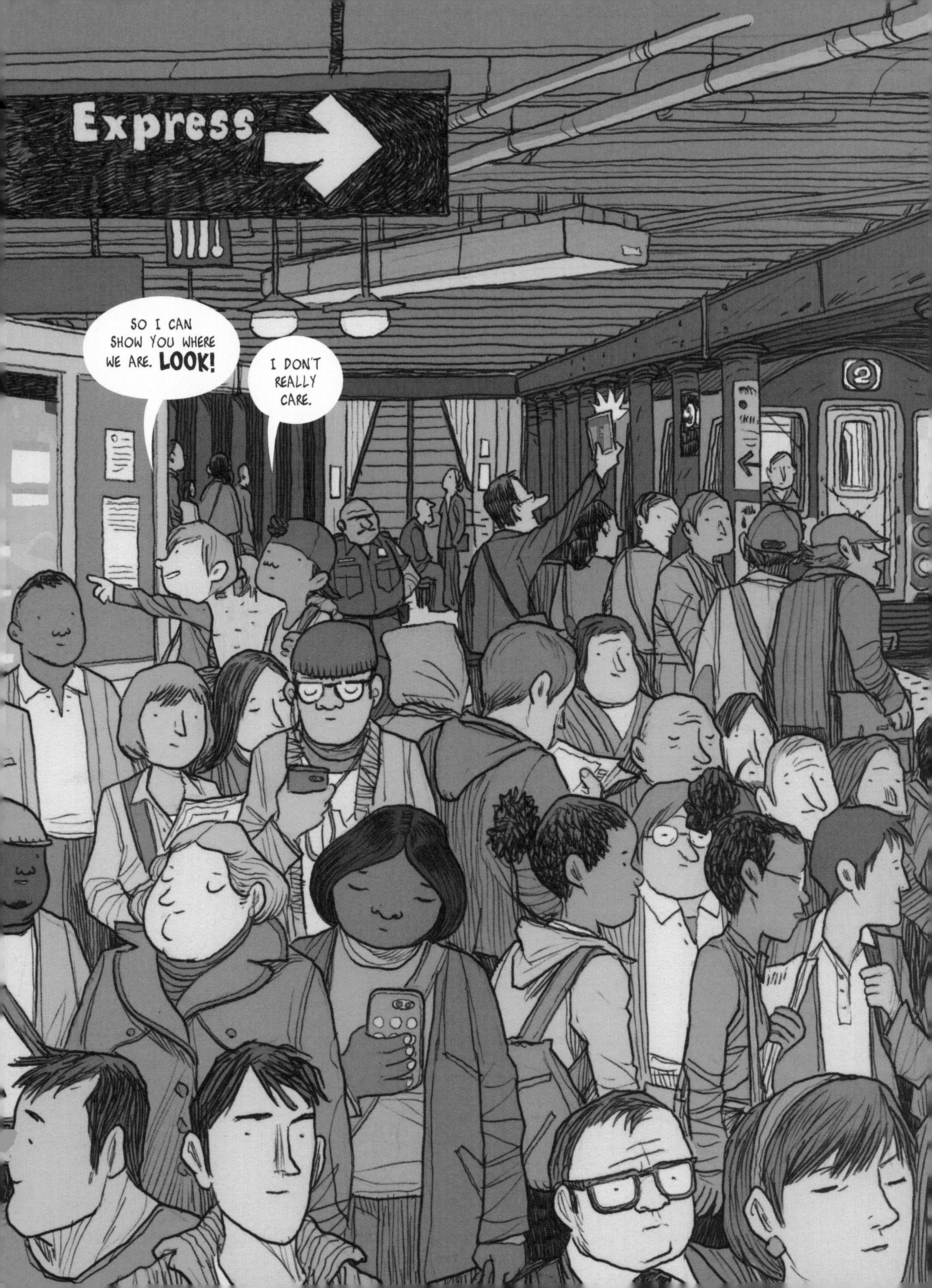
Express
SO I CAN SHOW YOU WHERE WE ARE. LOOK!
I DON'T REALLY CARE.

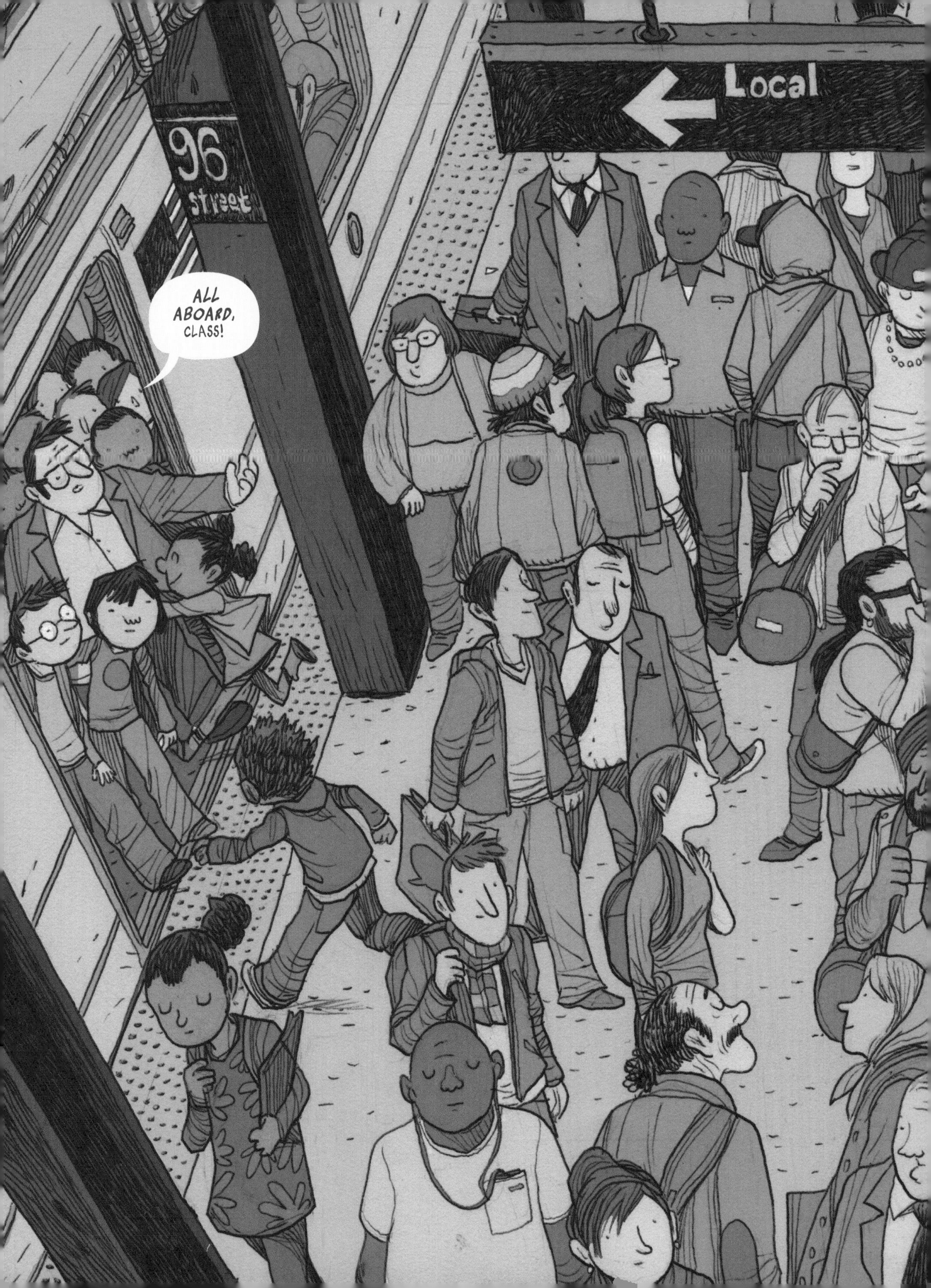
96
street
Local
ALL ABOARD, CLASS!

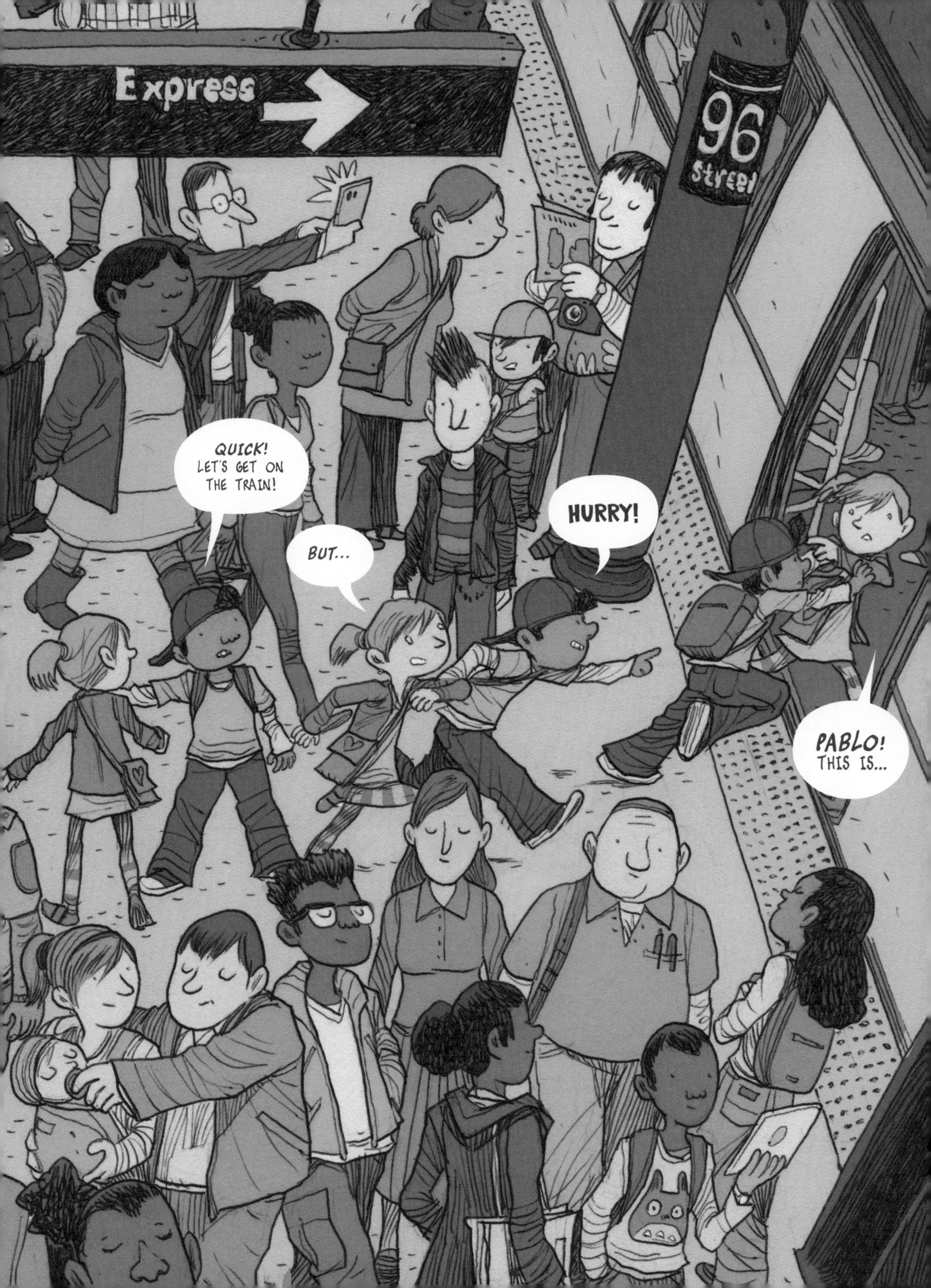
Express
96 Street
QUICK! LET'S GET ON THE TRAIN!
BUT...
HURRY!
PABLO! THIS IS...

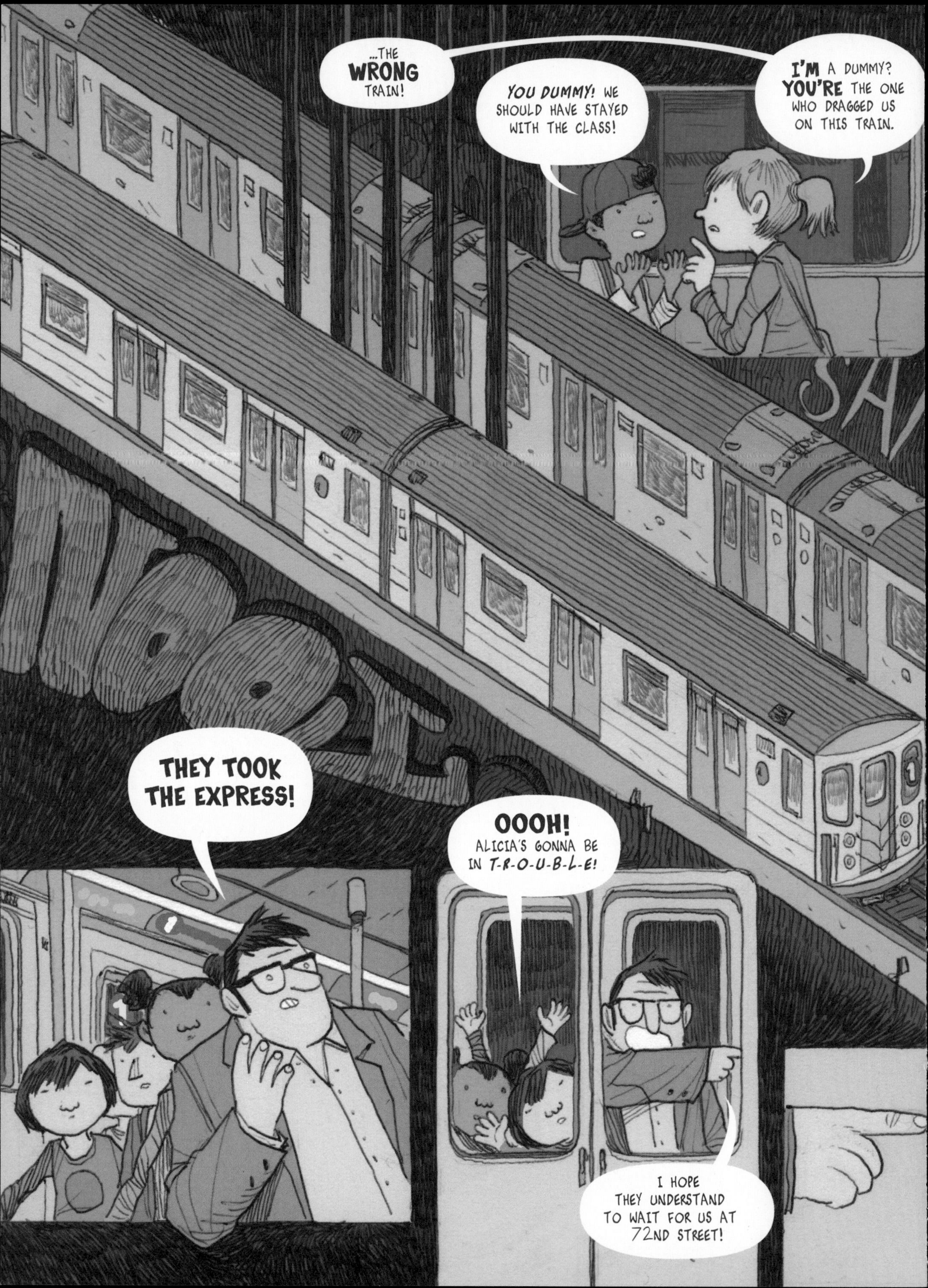
...THE WRONG TRAIN!
YOU DUMMY! WE SHOULD HAVE STAYED WITH THE CLASS!
I'M A DUMMY? YOU'RE THE ONE WHO DRAGGED US ON THIS TRAIN.
THEY TOOK THE EXPRESS!
OOOH! ALICIA'S GONNA BE IN T-R-O-U-B-L-E!
I HOPE THEY UNDERSTAND TO WAIT FOR US AT 72ND STREET!

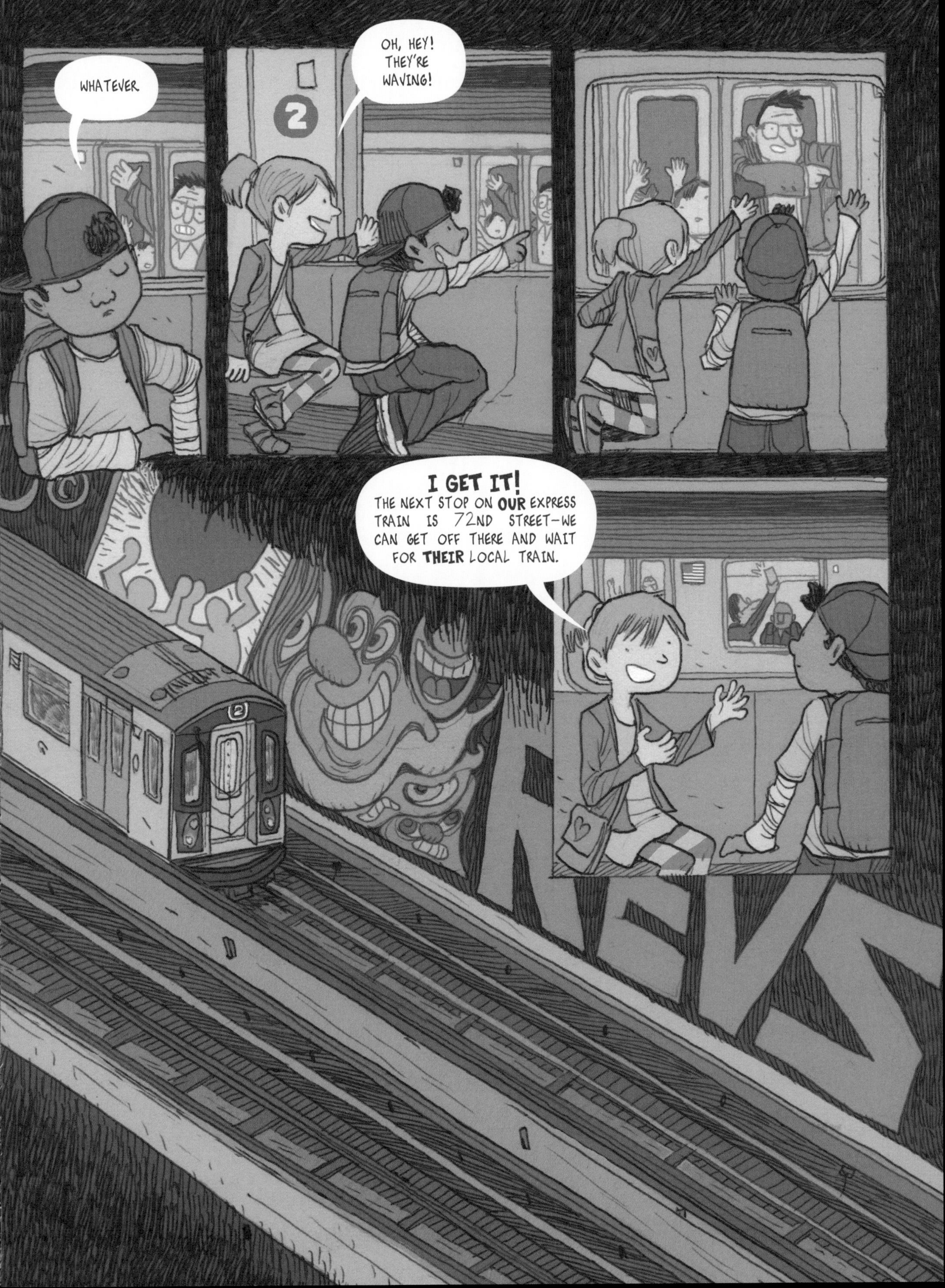
WHATEVER
OH, HEY! THEY'RE WAVING!
I GET IT! THE NEXT STOP ON OUR EXPRESS TRAIN IS 72ND STREET—WE CAN GET OFF THERE AND WAIT FOR THEIR LOCAL TRAIN.

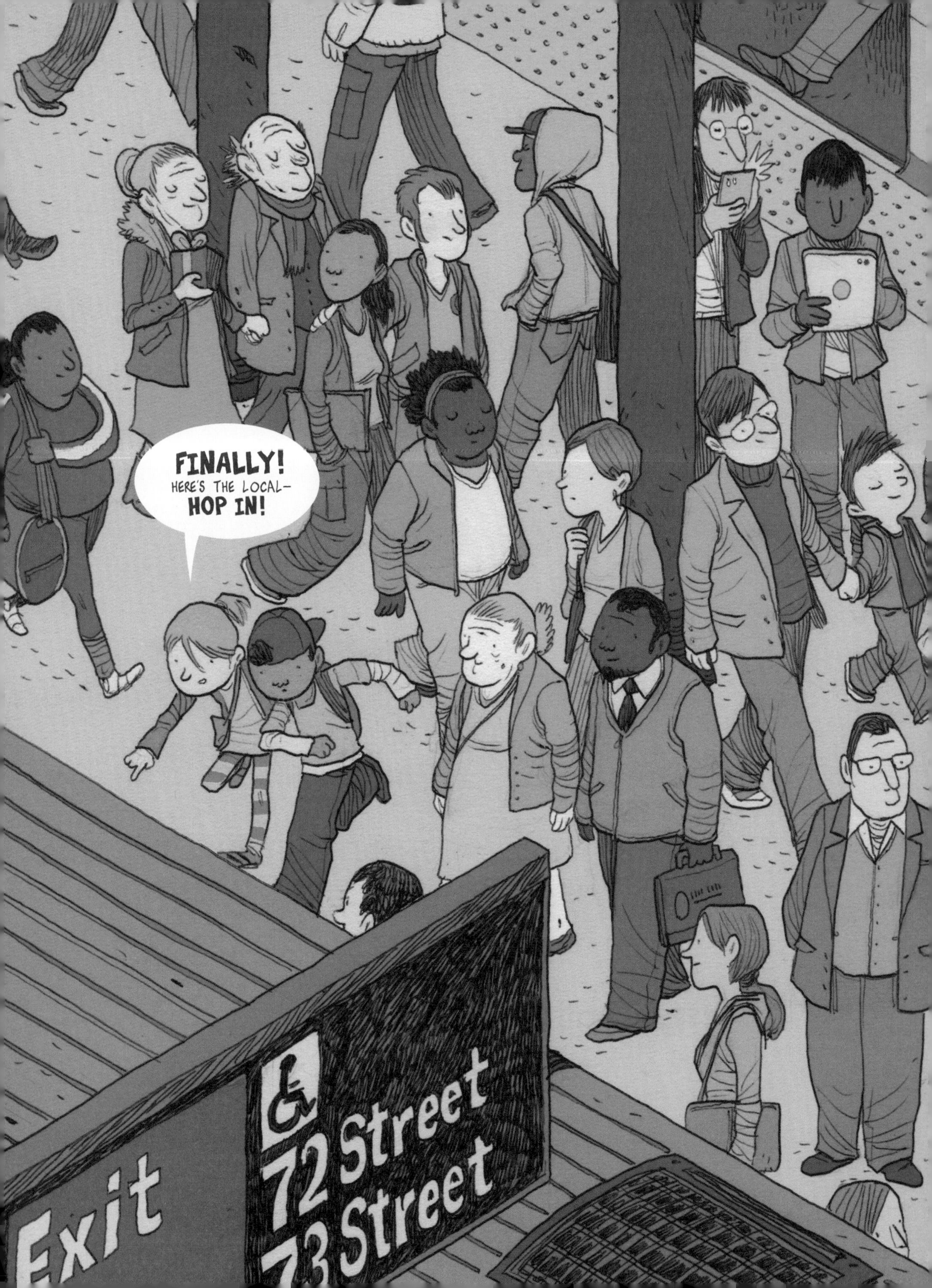
FINALLY! HERE'S THE LOCAL- HOP IN!
Exit
72 Street
73 Street

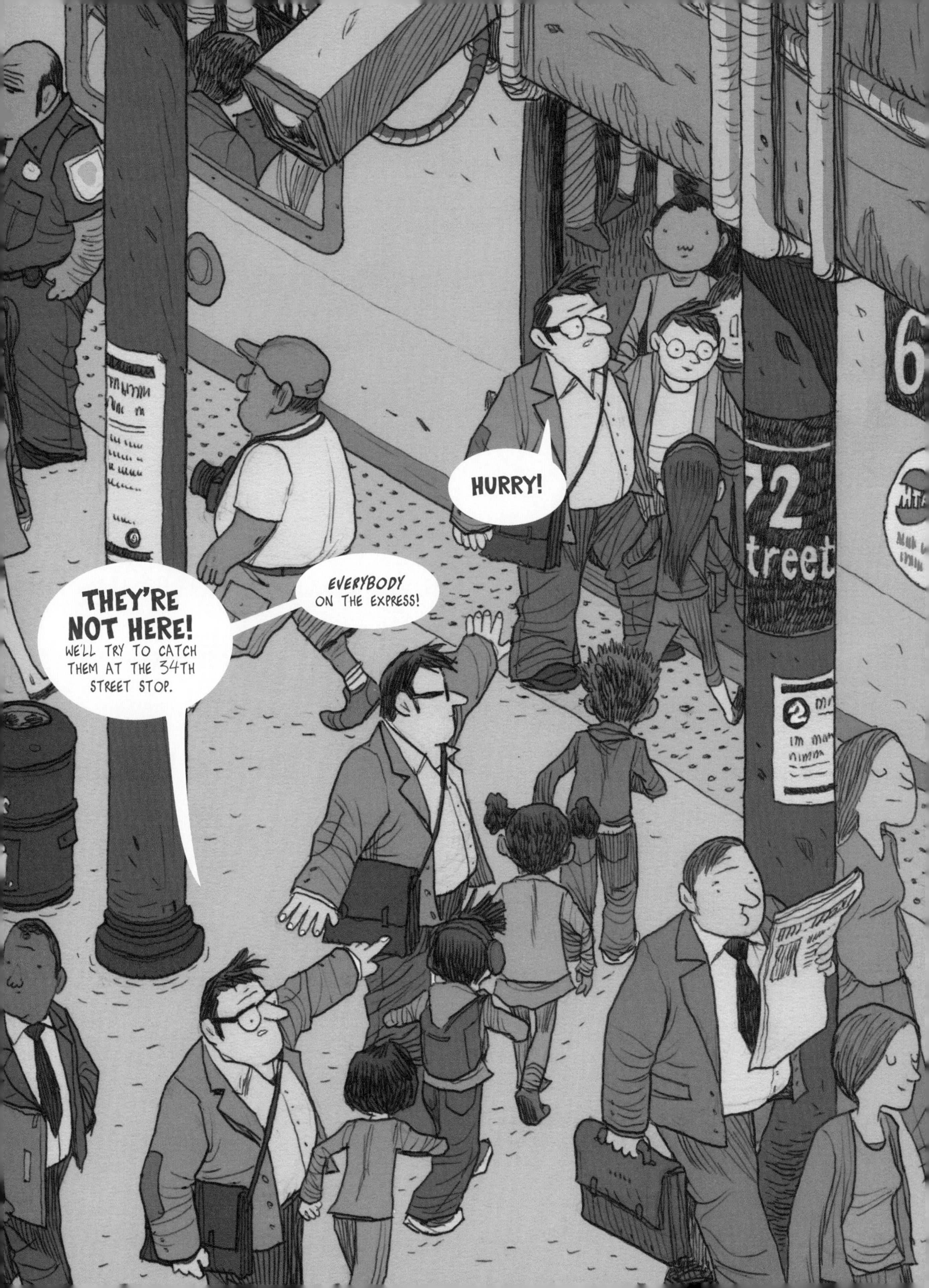
HURRY!
THEY'RE NOT HERE! WE'LL TRY TO CATCH THEM AT THE 34TH STREET STOP.
EVERYBODY ON THE EXPRESS!

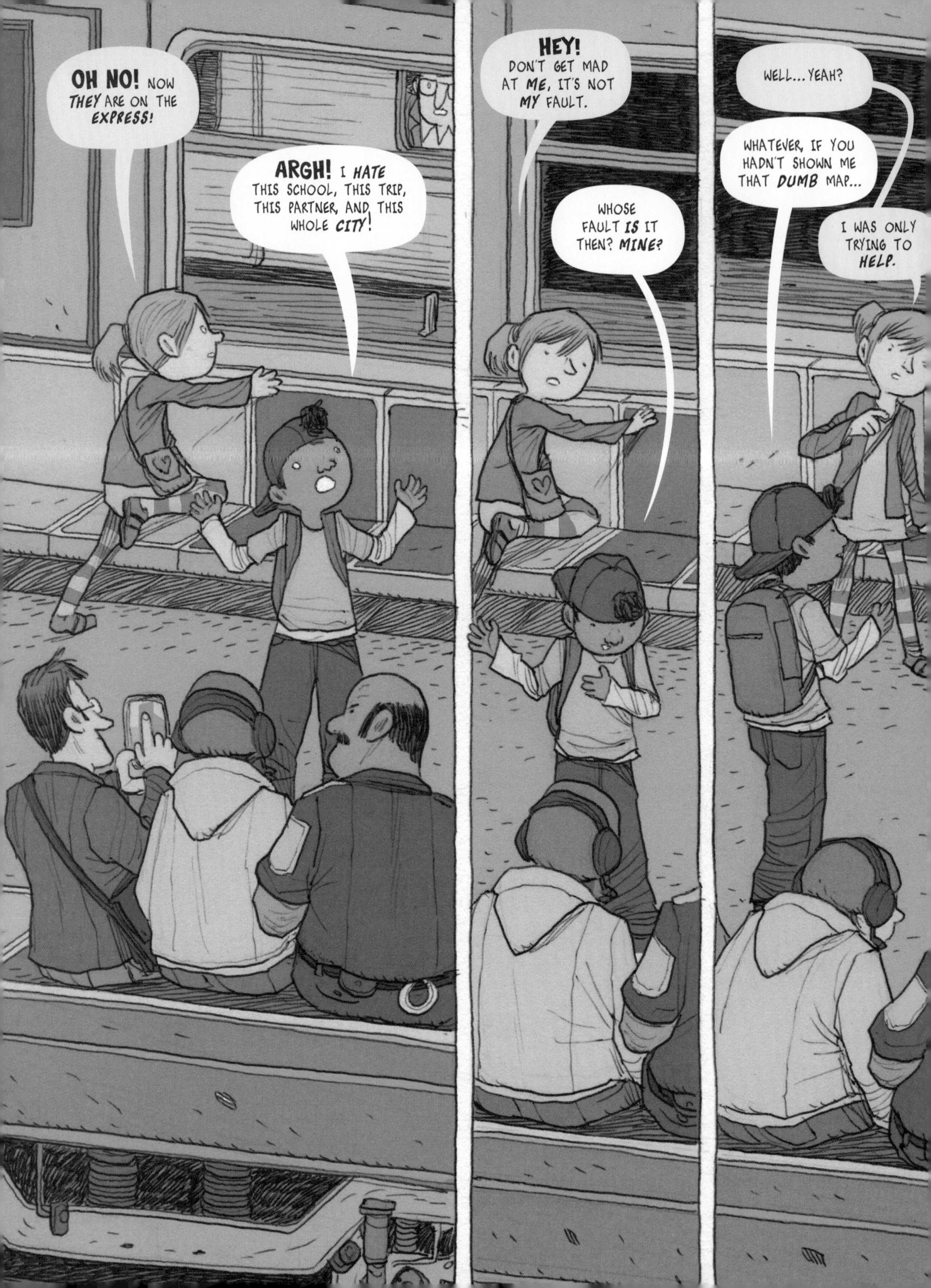

OH NO! NOW THEY ARE ON THE EXPRESS!
ARGH! I HATE THIS SCHOOL, THIS TRIP, THIS PARTNER, AND THIS WHOLE CITY!
HEY! DON'T GET MAD AT ME, IT'S NOT MY FAULT.
WHOSE FAULT IS IT THEN? MINE?
WELL... YEAH?
WHATEVER, IF YOU HADN'T SHOWN ME THAT DUMB MAP...
I WAS ONLY TRYING TO HELP.

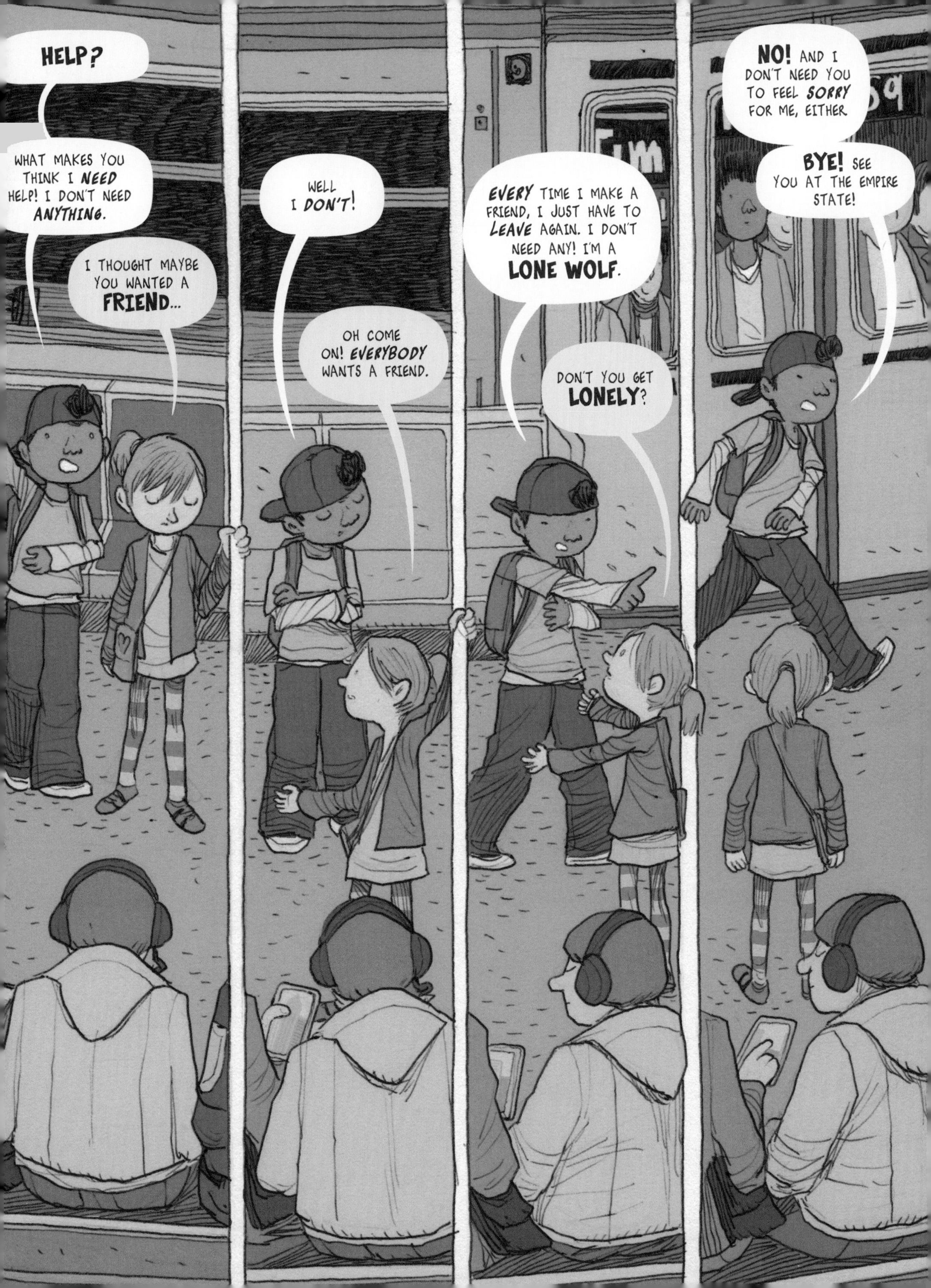
HELP?
WHAT MAKES YOU THINK I NEED HELP! I DON'T NEED ANYTHING.
I THOUGHT MAYBE YOU WANTED A FRIEND...
WELL I DON'T!
OH COME ON! EVERYBODY WANTS A FRIEND.
EVERY TIME I MAKE A FRIEND, I JUST HAVE TO LEAVE AGAIN. I DON'T NEED ANY! I'M A LONE WOLF.
DON'T YOU GET LONELY?
NO! AND I DON'T NEED YOU TO FEEL SORRY FOR ME, EITHER
BYE! SEE YOU AT THE EMPIRE STATE!

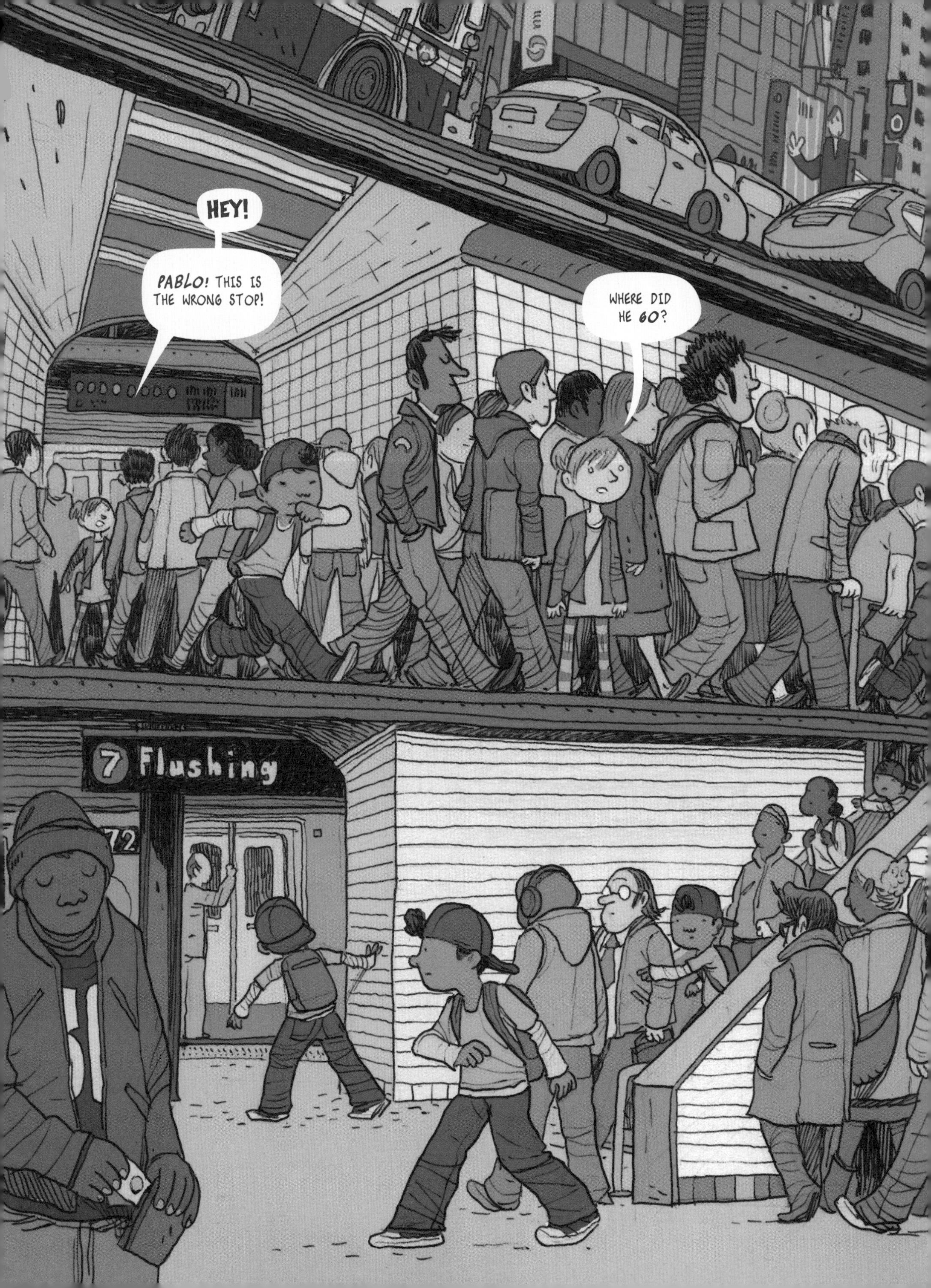
HEY!
PABLO! THIS IS THE WRONG STOP!
WHERE DID HE GO?
7 Flushing

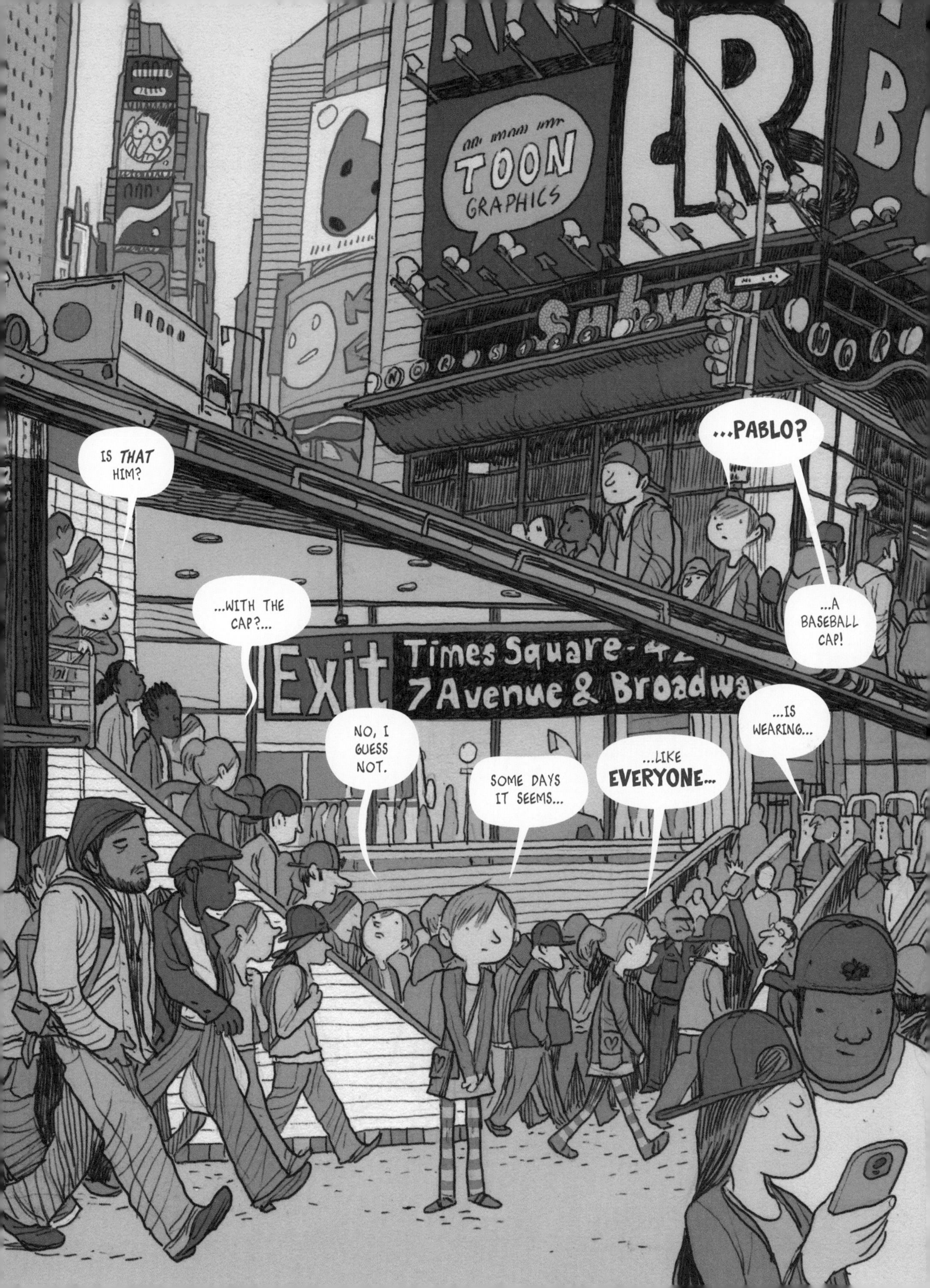
TOON
GRAPHICS
Exit
Times Square-
7 Avenue &
IS *THAT* HIM?
...WITH THE CAP?...
NO, I GUESS NOT.
SOME DAYS IT SEEMS...
...LIKE **EVERYONE...**
...IS WEARING...
...A BASEBALL CAP!
...PABLO?

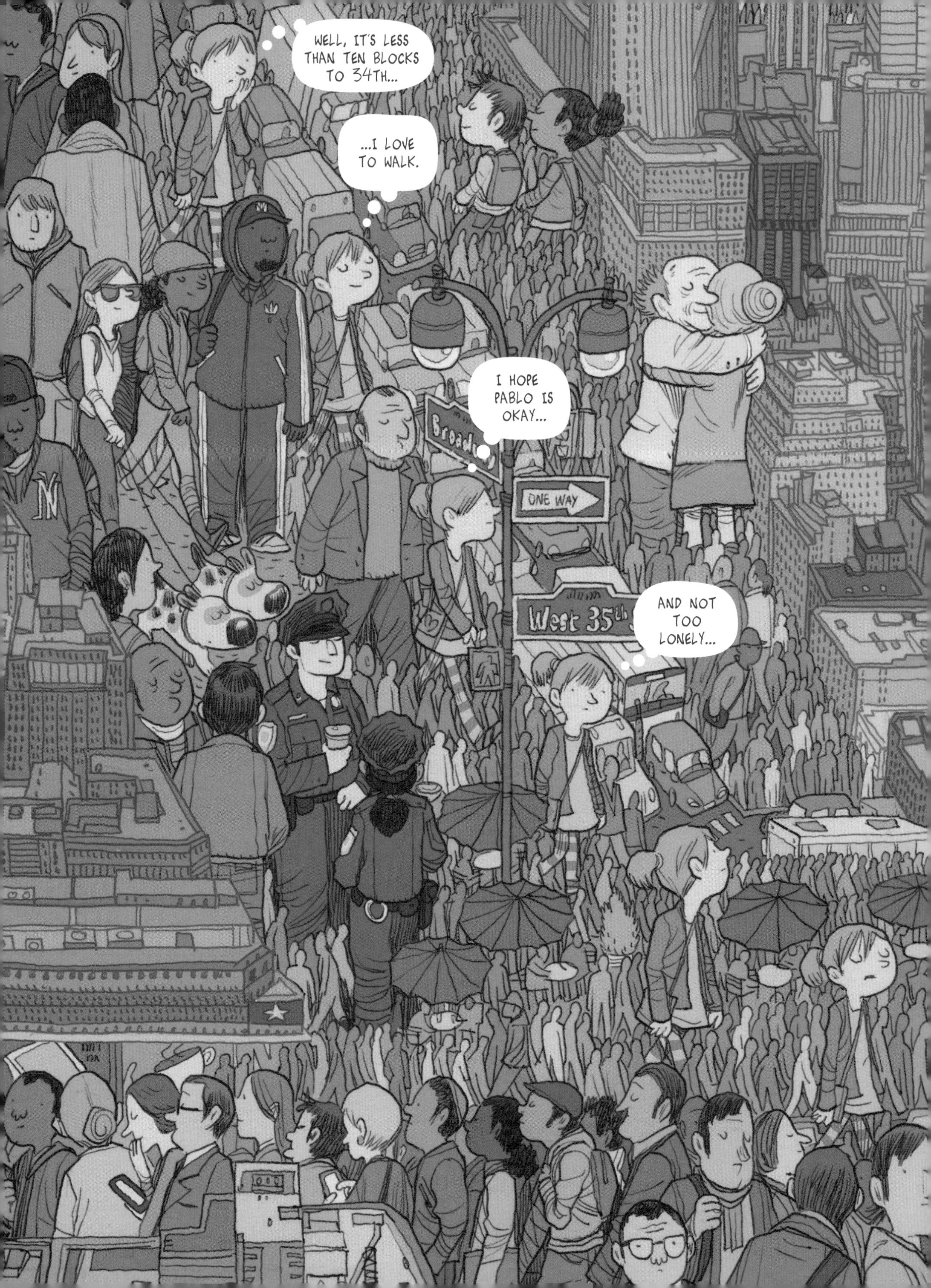
WELL, IT'S LESS THAN TEN BLOCKS TO 34TH...
...I LOVE TO WALK.
Broadway
ONE WAY
I HOPE PABLO IS OKAY...
West 35th
AND NOT TOO LONELY...

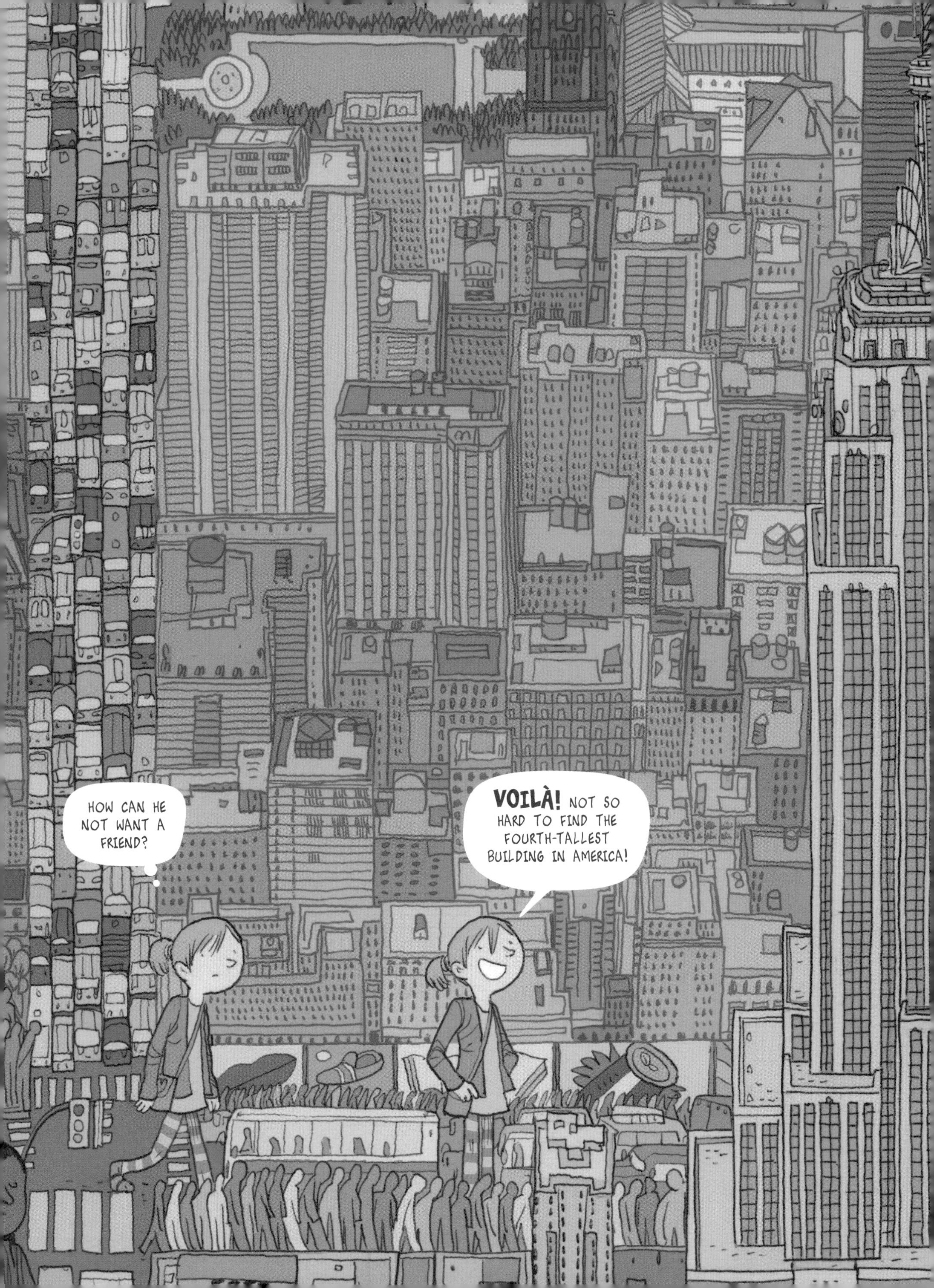

HOW CAN HE NOT WANT A FRIEND?
VOILÀ! NOT SO HARD TO FIND THE FOURTH-TALLEST BUILDING IN AMERICA!

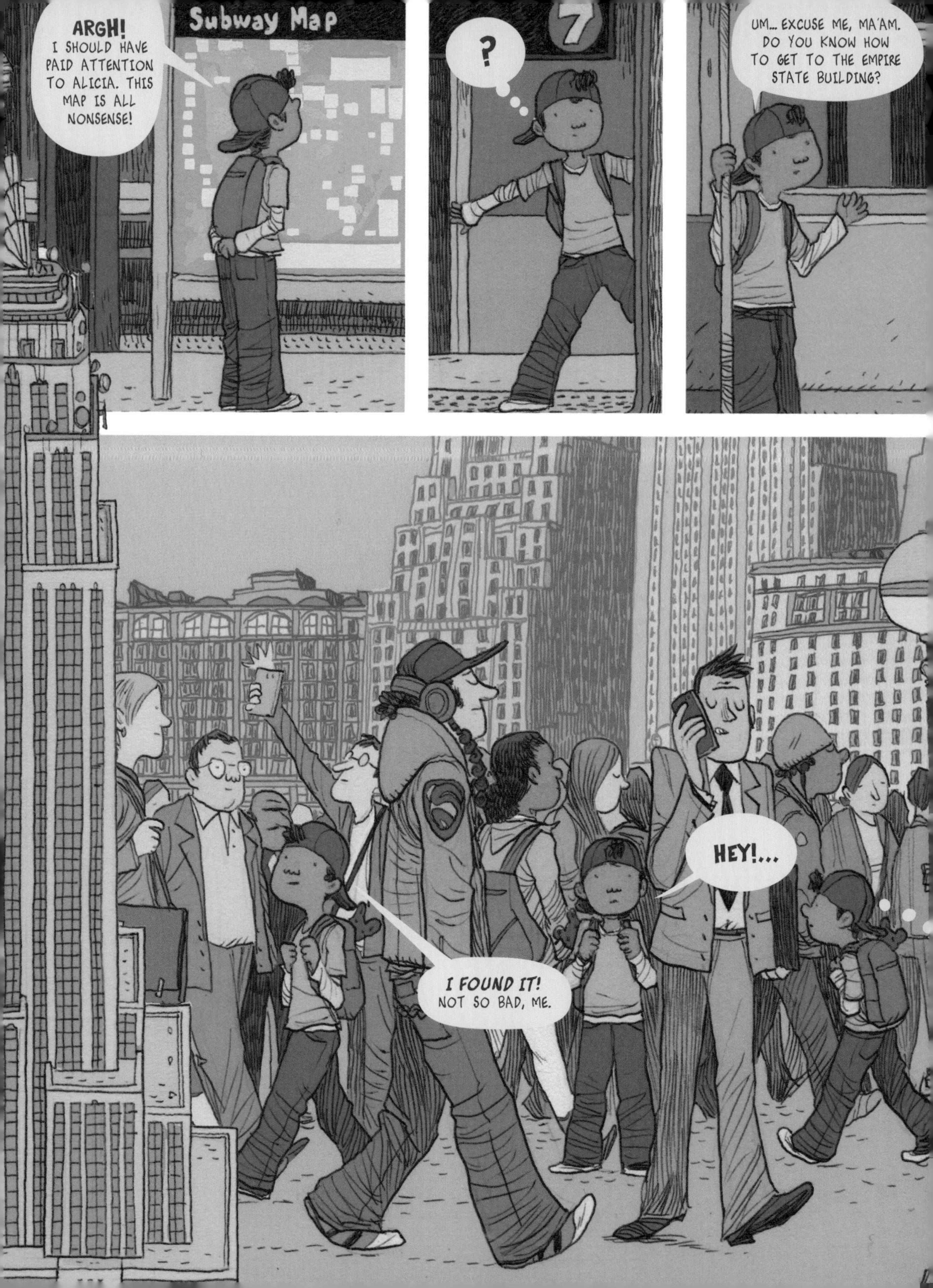

Subway Map
ARGH! I SHOULD HAVE PAID ATTENTION TO ALICIA. THIS MAP IS ALL NONSENSE!
7
?
UM... EXCUSE ME, MA'AM. DO YOU KNOW HOW TO GET TO THE EMPIRE STATE BUILDING?
HEY!...
I FOUND IT! NOT SO BAD, ME.

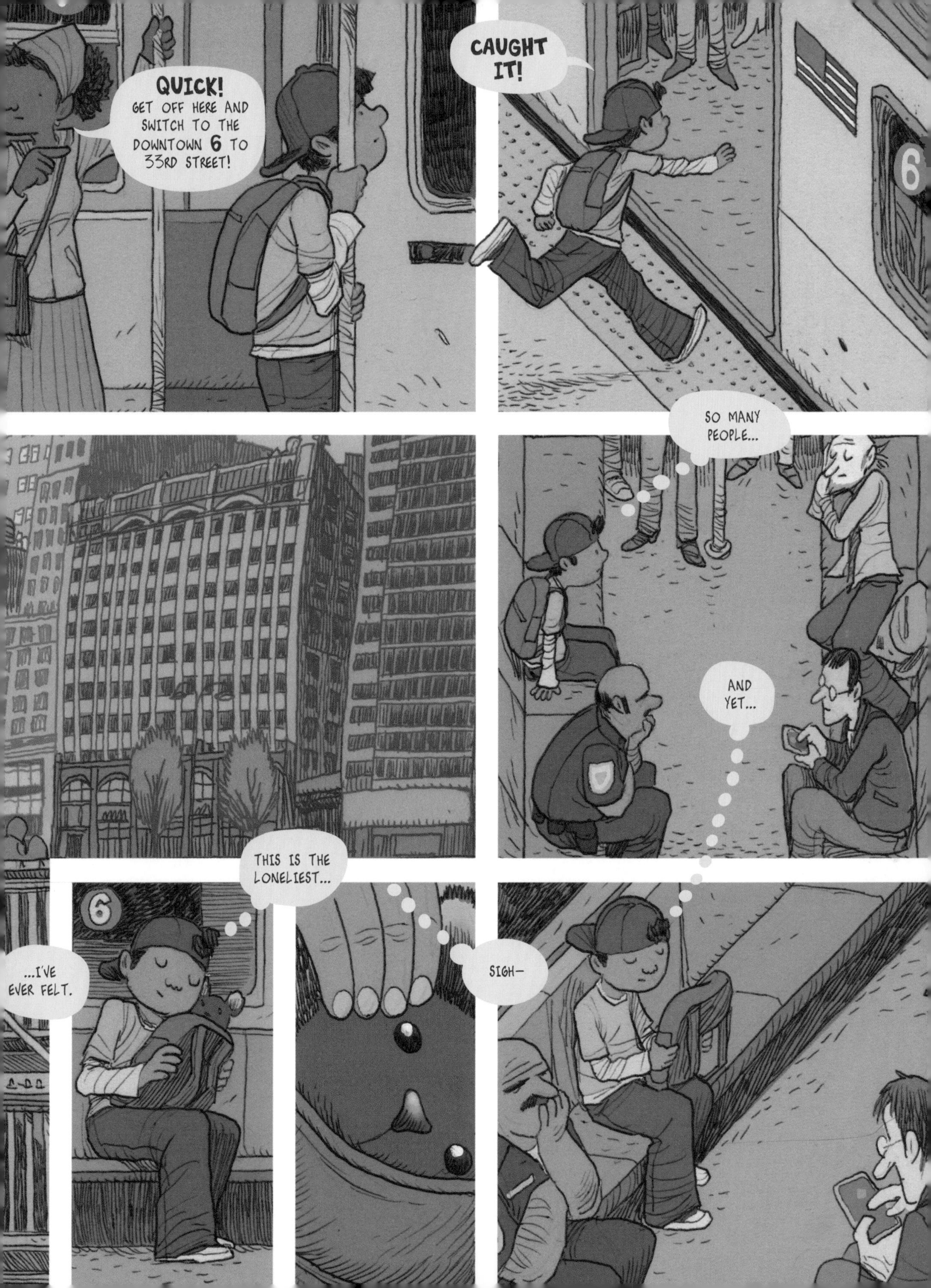
QUICK! GET OFF HERE AND SWITCH TO THE DOWNTOWN 6 TO 33RD STREET!
CAUGHT IT!
6
SO MANY PEOPLE...
AND YET...
THIS IS THE LONELIEST...
...I'VE EVER FELT.
6
SIGH—

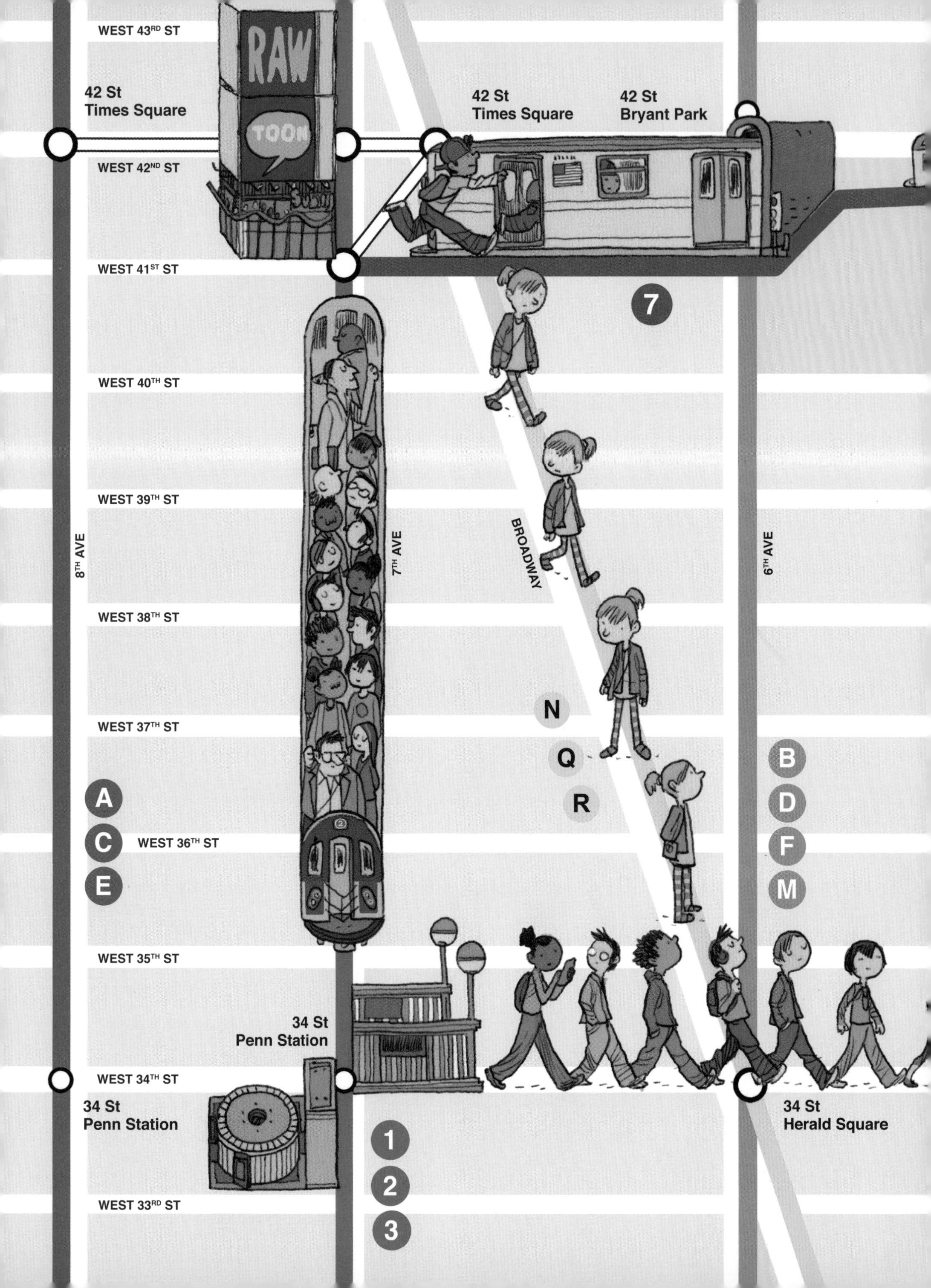

WEST 43RD ST
RAW
TOON
42 St
Times Square
42 St
Times Square
42 St
Bryant Park
WEST 42ND ST
WEST 41ST ST
7
WEST 40TH ST
WEST 39TH ST
8TH AVE
7TH AVE
BROADWAY
6TH AVE
WEST 38TH ST
N
WEST 37TH ST
Q
B
A
R
D
C
WEST 36TH ST
F
E
M
WEST 35TH ST
34 St
Penn Station
WEST 34TH ST
34 St
Penn Station
34 St
Herald Square
1
2
WEST 33RD ST
3

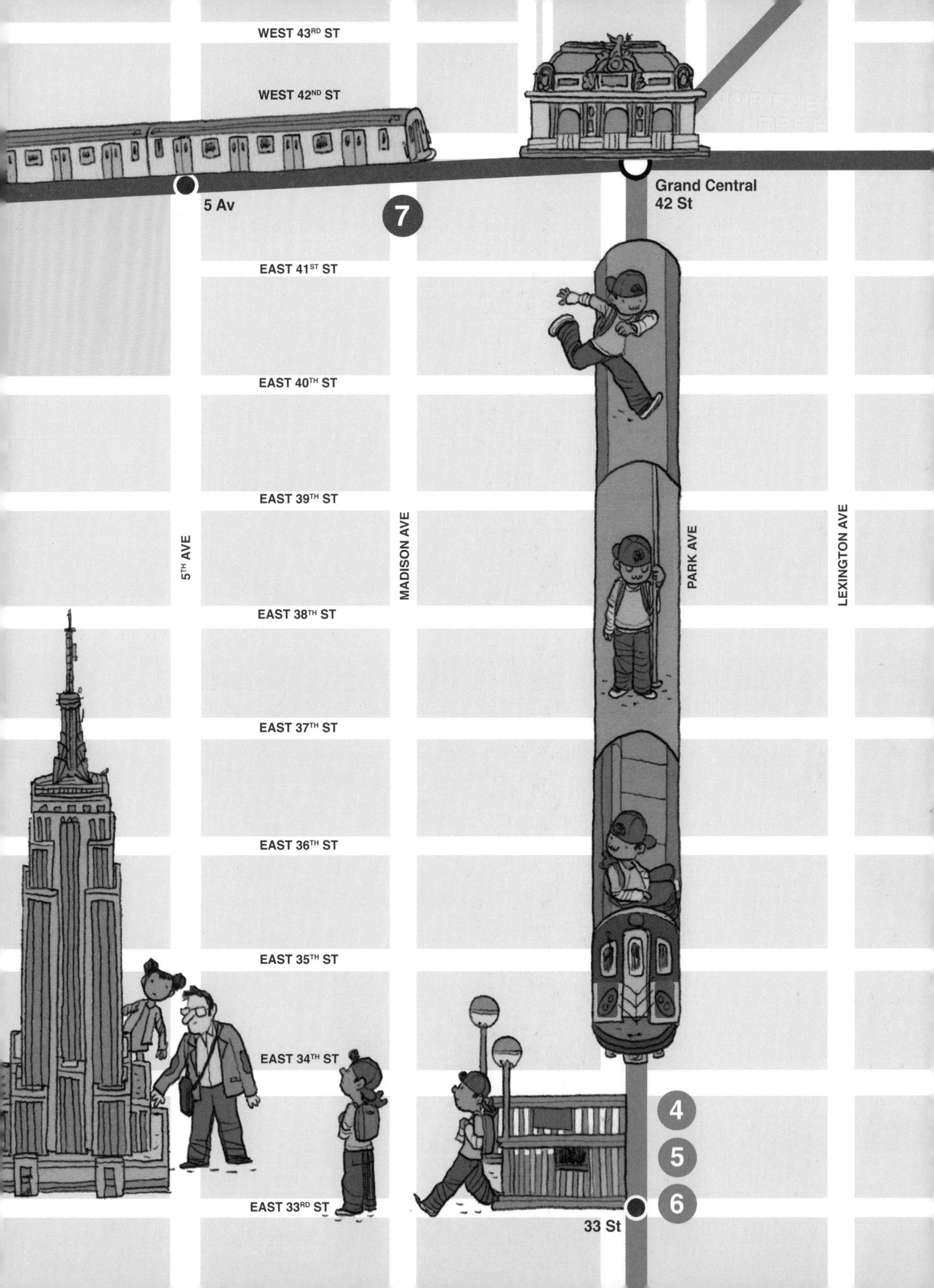
WEST 43RD ST
WEST 42ND ST
5 Av
7
Grand Central
42 St
EAST 41ST ST
EAST 40TH ST
EAST 39TH ST
5TH AVE
MADISON AVE
PARK AVE
LEXINGTON AVE
EAST 38TH ST
EAST 37TH ST
EAST 36TH ST
EAST 35TH ST
EAST 34TH ST
4
5
6
EAST 33RD ST
33 St

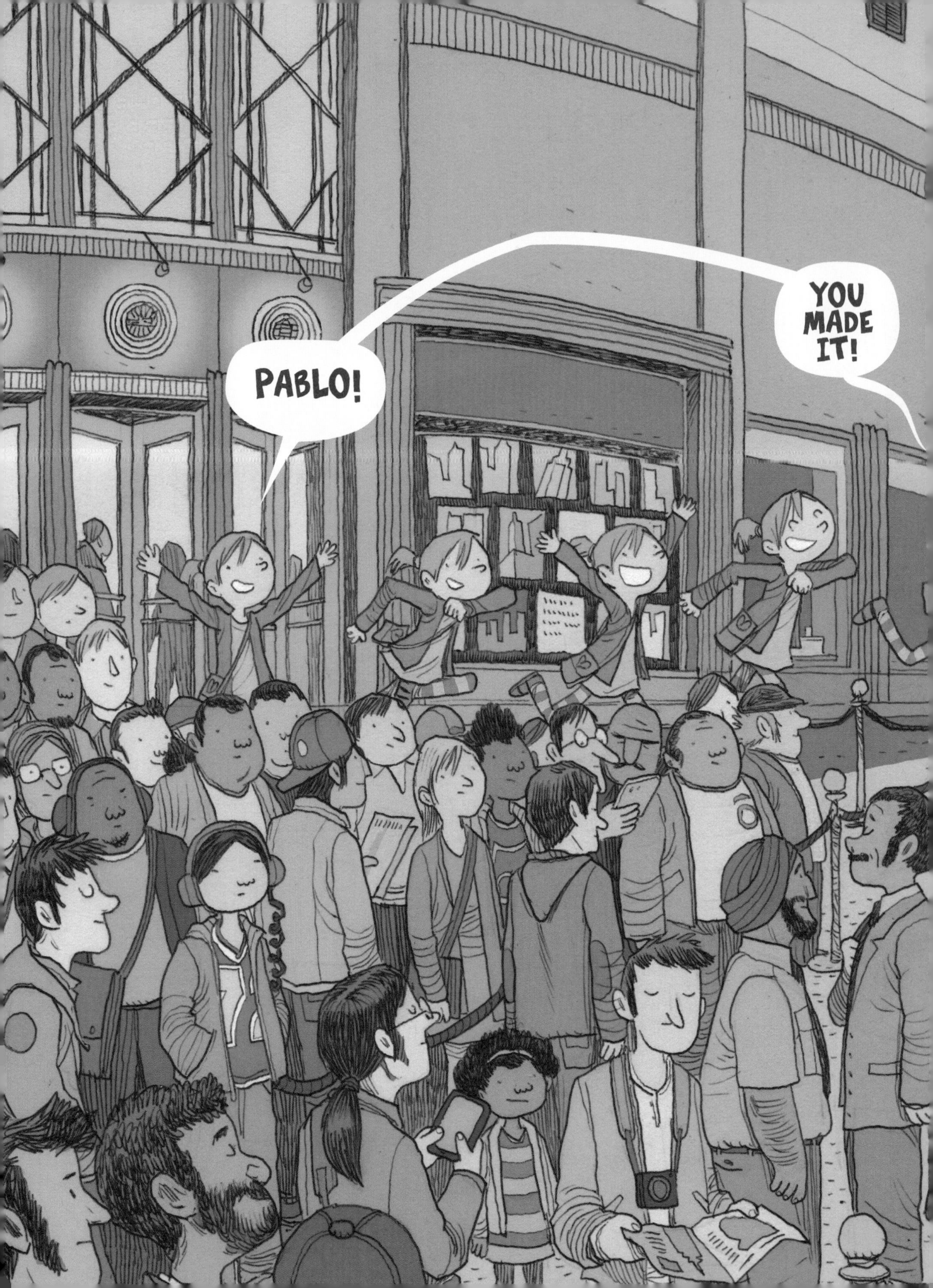
PABLO!
YOU MADE IT!

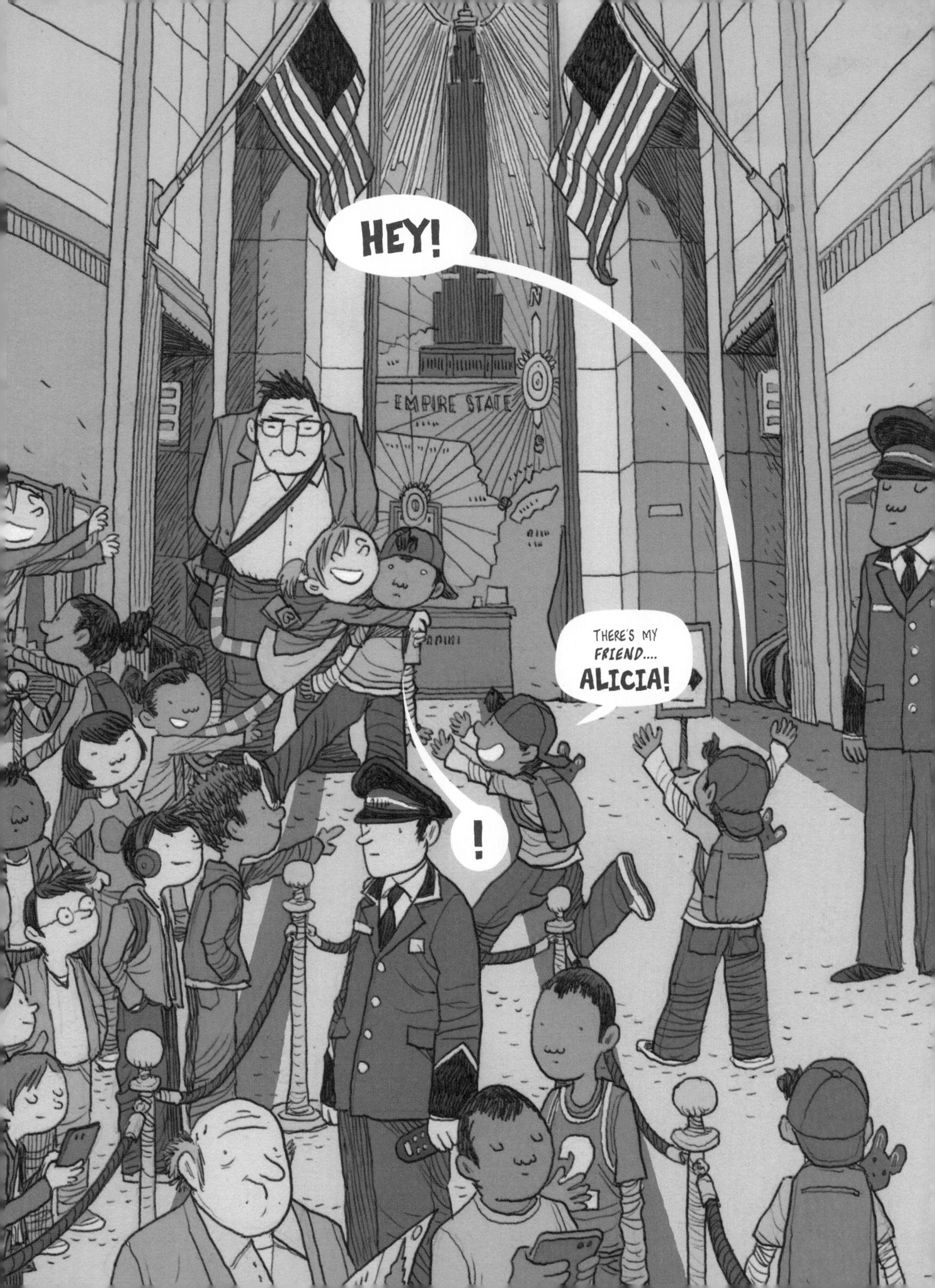
HEY!
EMPIRE STATE
THERE'S MY FRIEND.... ALICIA!
!

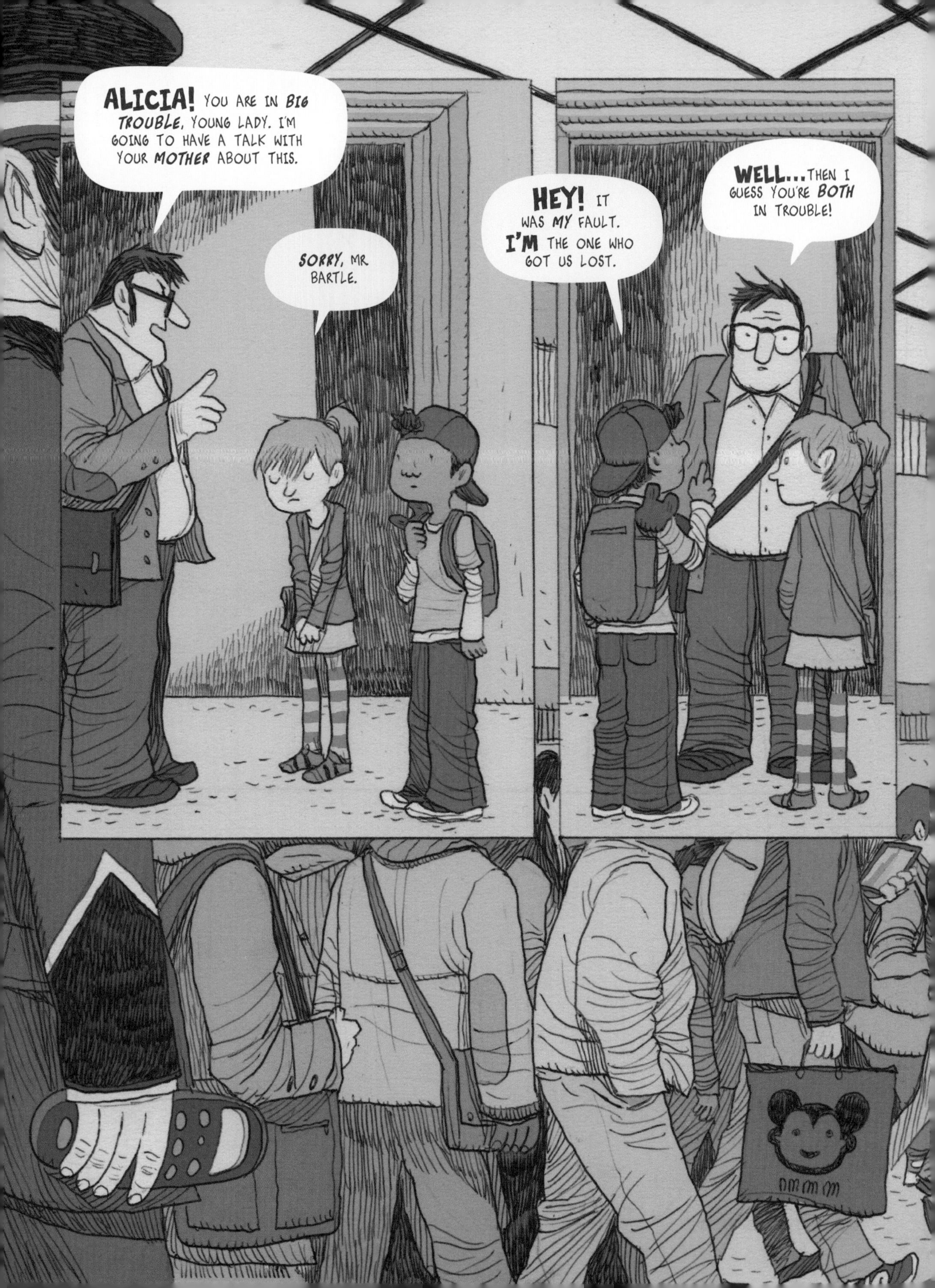
ALICIA! YOU ARE IN BIG TROUBLE, YOUNG LADY. I'M GOING TO HAVE A TALK WITH YOUR MOTHER ABOUT THIS.
SORRY, MR BARTLE.
HEY! IT WAS MY FAULT. I'M THE ONE WHO GOT US LOST.
WELL... THEN I GUESS YOU'RE BOTH IN TROUBLE!

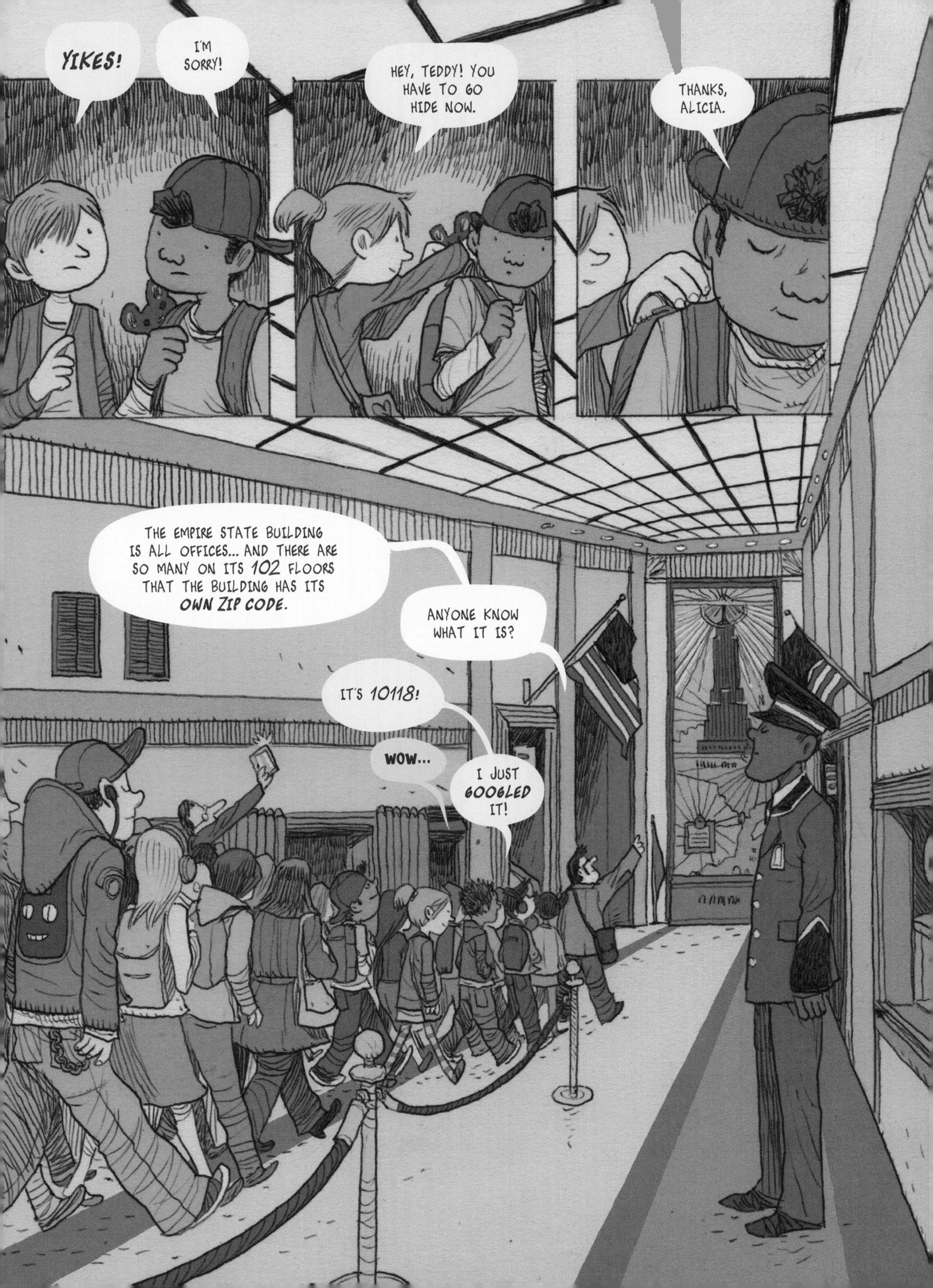
YIKES!
I'M SORRY!
HEY, TEDDY! YOU HAVE TO GO HIDE NOW.
THANKS, ALICIA.
THE EMPIRE STATE BUILDING IS ALL OFFICES... AND THERE ARE SO MANY ON ITS 102 FLOORS THAT THE BUILDING HAS ITS OWN ZIP CODE.
ANYONE KNOW WHAT IT IS?
IT'S 10118!
WOW...
I JUST GOOGLED IT!

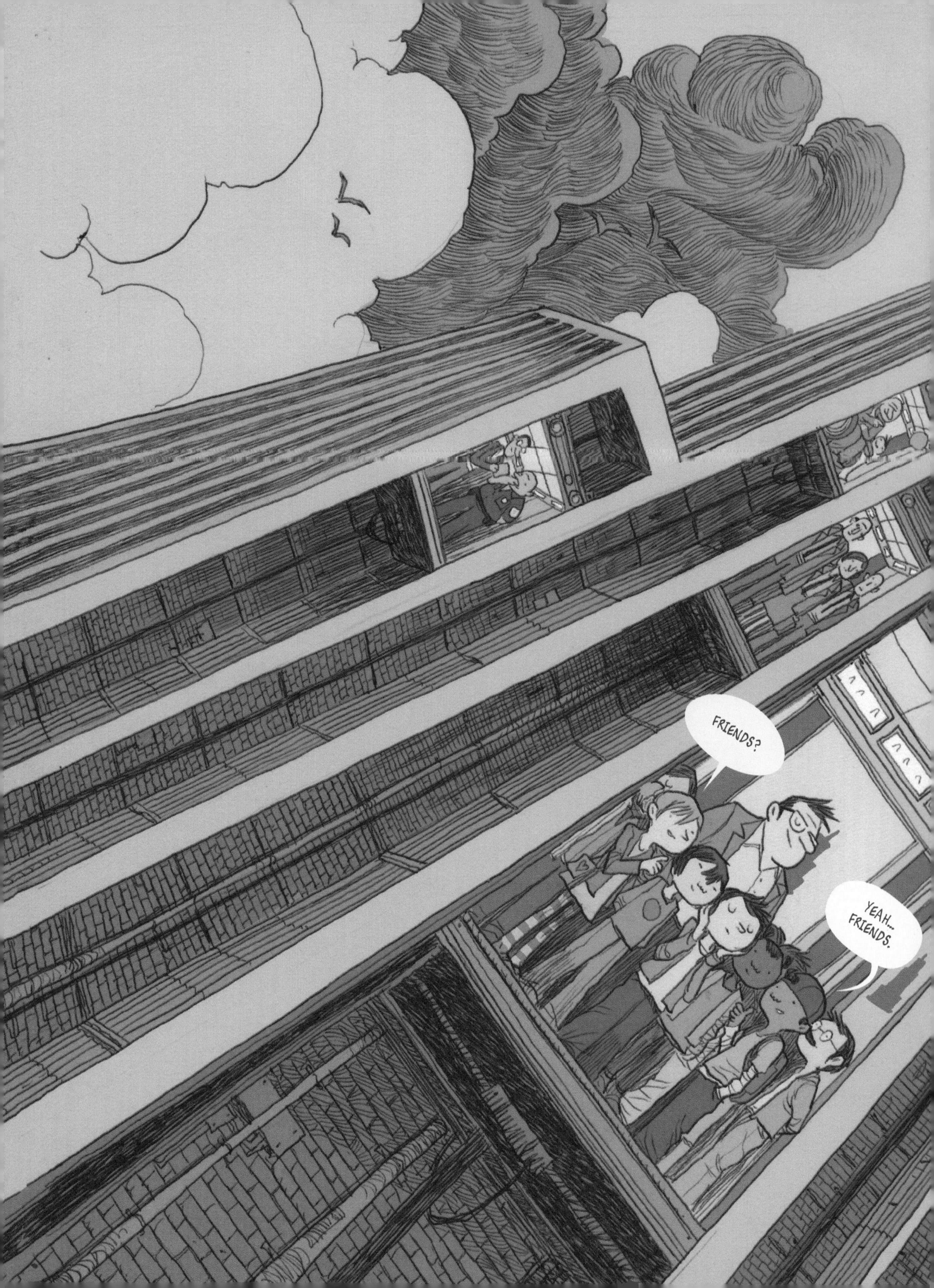
FRIENDS?
YEAH... FRIENDS.

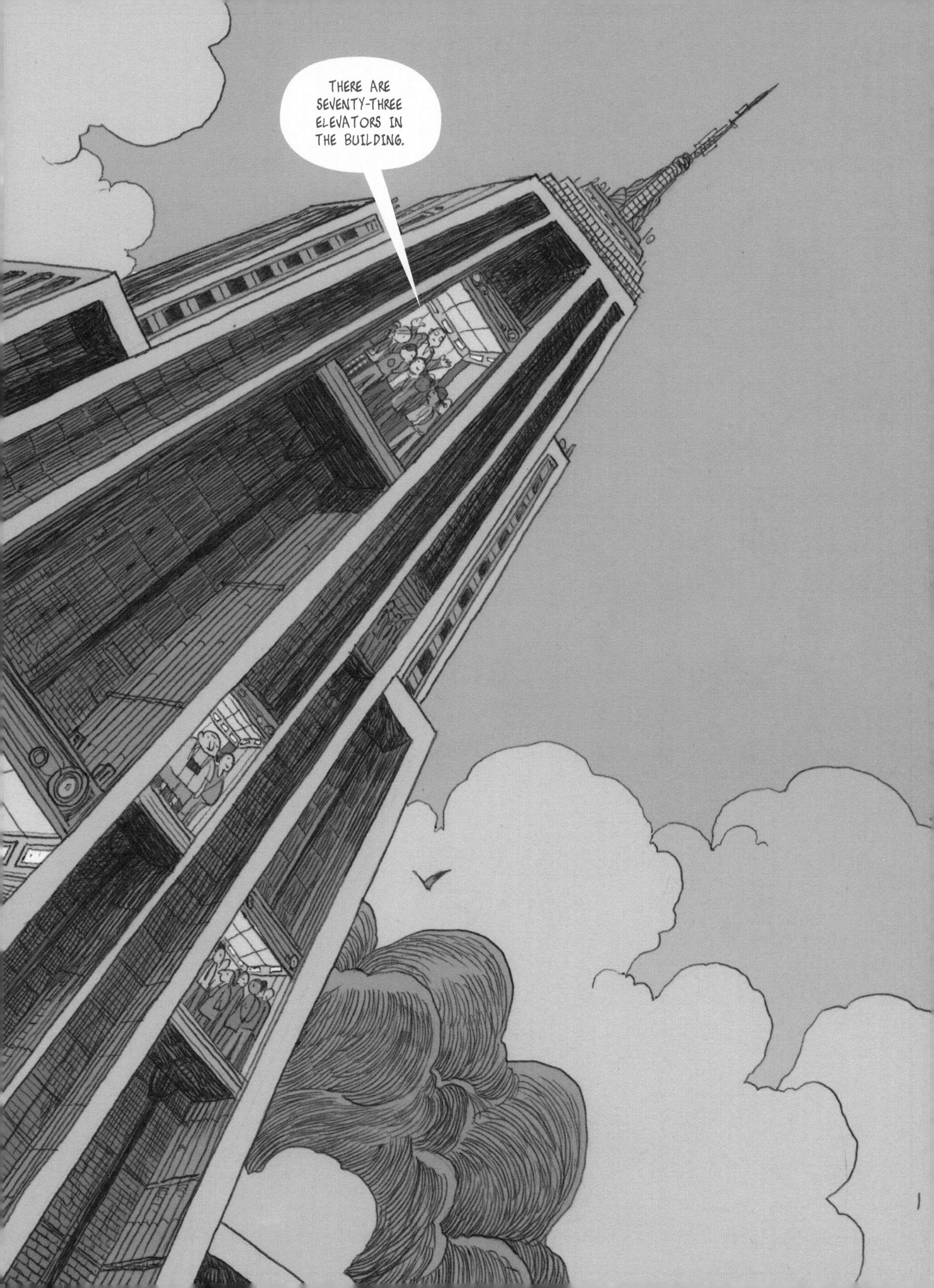
THERE ARE SEVENTY-THREE ELEVATORS IN THE BUILDING.

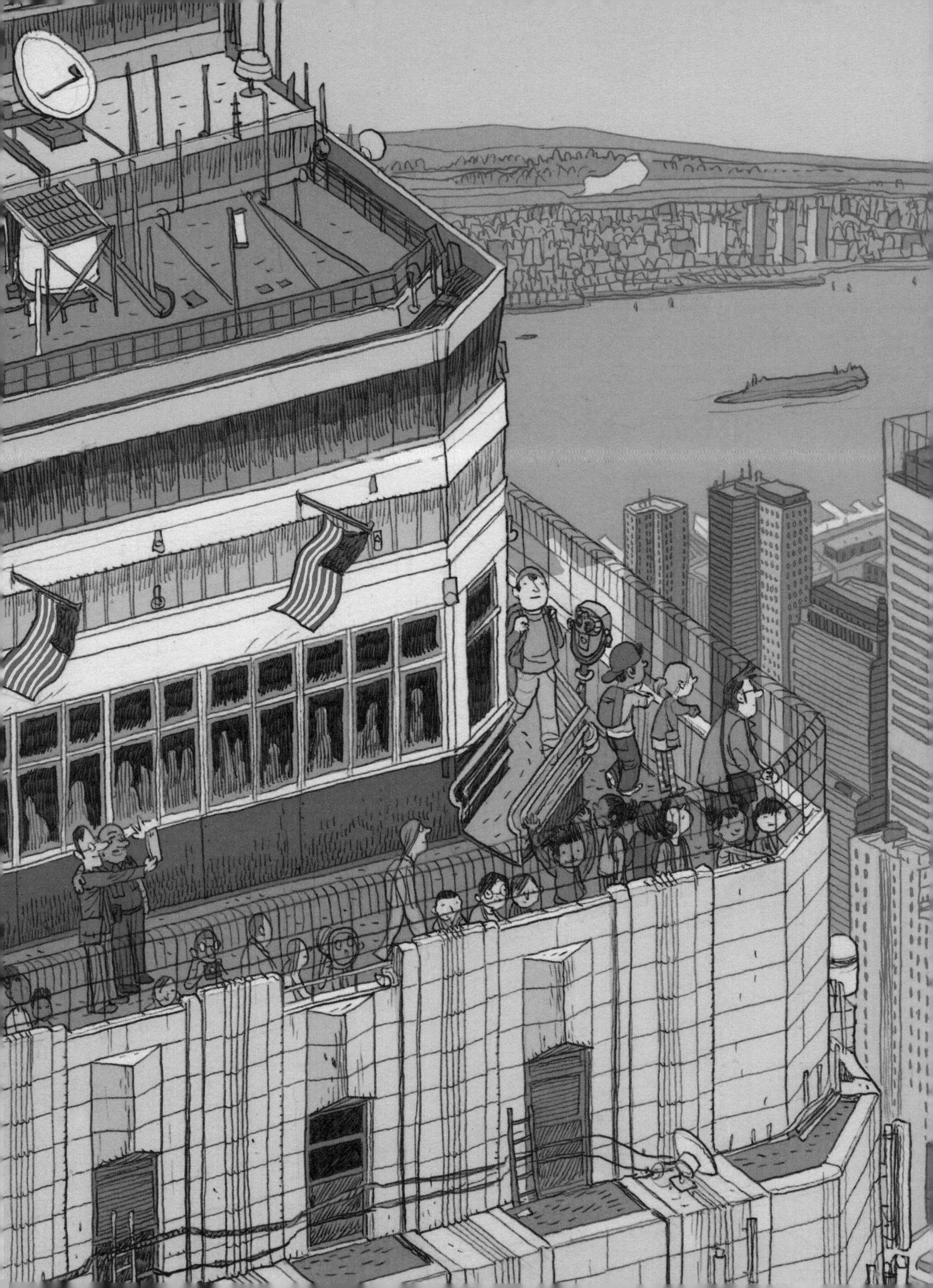

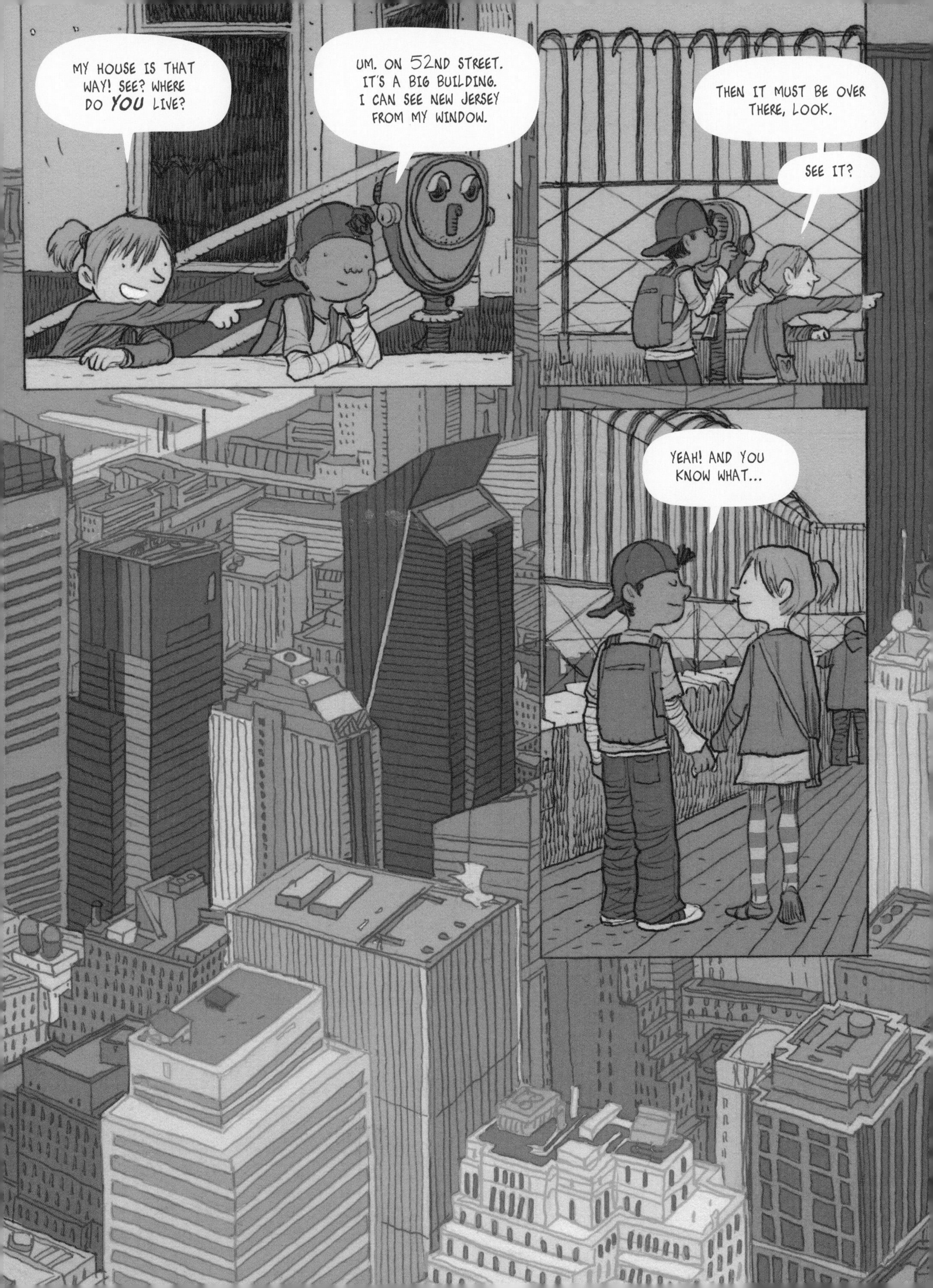

MY HOUSE IS THAT WAY! SEE? WHERE DO *YOU* LIVE?
UM. ON 52ND STREET. IT'S A BIG BUILDING. I CAN SEE NEW JERSEY FROM MY WINDOW.
THEN IT MUST BE OVER THERE, LOOK.
SEE IT?
YEAH! AND YOU KNOW WHAT...

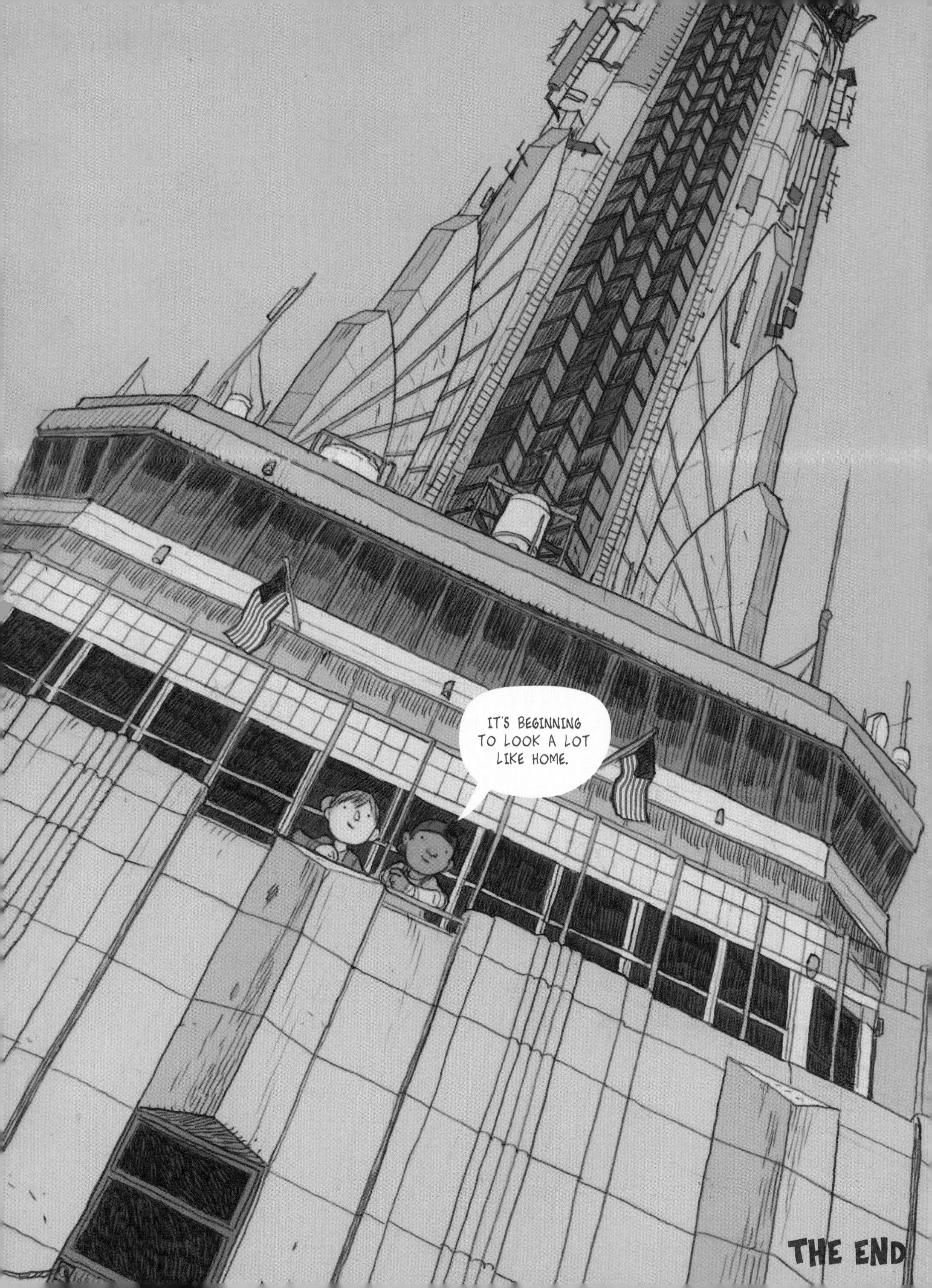
IT'S BEGINNING TO LOOK A LOT LIKE HOME.
THE END

ABOUT THE AUTHORS

NADJA SPIEGELMAN is the Eisner Award-nominated author of the Zig and Wikki series of science comics for young children. She is a native New Yorker, who prides herself on important subway know-how, such as where to stand to get a seat, and how to sleep without missing her stop. She began taking the subway alone when she was eleven years old. Her favorite train is the Q train because it goes on a bridge over the East River, and the view of the Manhattan skyline is beautiful every time.

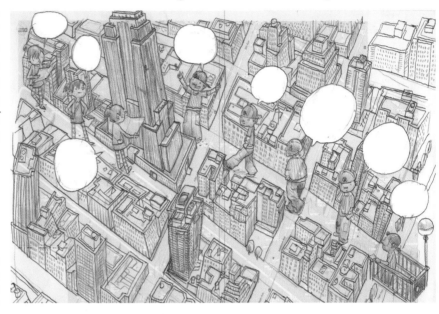

One of the many preparatory sketches made by the artist.

SERGIO GARCÍA SÁNCHEZ, a professor of comics in Angoulême, France and at the University of Granada, Spain, is one of Europe's most celebrated experimental cartoonists. His work has been published in over forty-five books and translated into nine languages. He lives in Granada with his wife and collaborator, Lola Moral, who colored the art for this book and provided the translation for the Spanish edition, *Perdidos en NYC: Una Aventura en el Metro*. They have two children, Pablo and Alicia.

BEHIND THE SCENES: SERGIO AND THE COP

 This is Sergio's first book published in the U.S. and is based on his first trip to New York City. He filled notebook after notebook with sketches and rode the subway for days. When he went into the 96th Street subway station, he began photographing all the details he knew he would need: the vending machines, the turnstiles, and the signs. At  some point, he realized that he had attracted the attention of a cop, so he hurried down the stairs. Once on the platform, he started taking pictures again. Turning around, he spotted someone in his view screen…the cop who had been following him! Fortunately, a train was entering the station at that moment. As soon as the doors opened, Sergio jumped in, eager to escape the unwanted attention. To celebrate his own adventure, Sergio decided to show himself and the cop in virtually every spread of this book. Hop on a subway with them and enjoy the behind-the-scenes adventure!

THE BEGINNINGS OF THE SUBWAY

By the late 1800s, when talk of a subway system began, public transit in New York City was already thriving. There were trains, ferries, and many horse-drawn carriages. What it lacked, however, was unification and efficiency. The roads in New York City were largely unpaved and plagued by street congestion. Transportation had to move off the street. The first attempt was in 1867, when a self-trained engineer named Charles T. Harvey built the first elevated train line, nicknamed the "one-legged railroad" because it ran on a single track! Service on the line was initially provided by cable cars, but they were replaced four years later by steam locomotives.

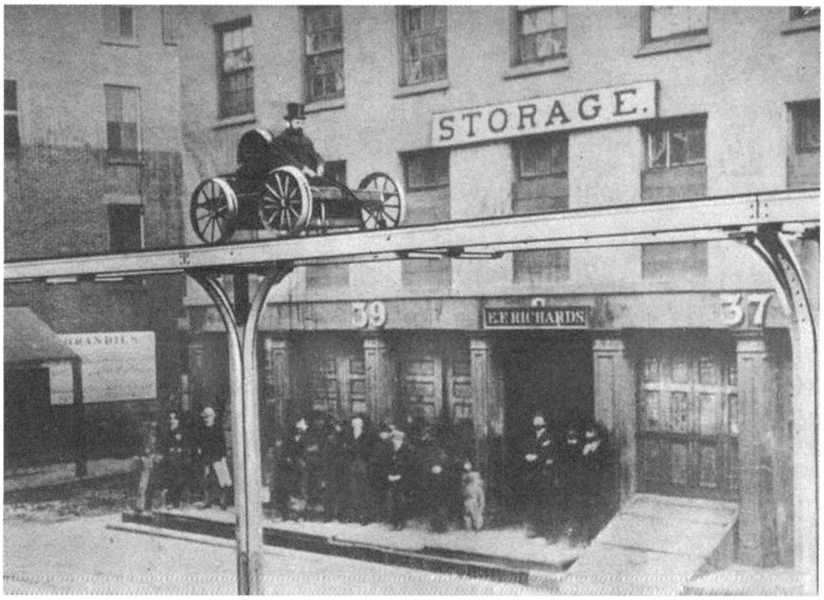
STORAGE.
39
E.F.RICHARDS
37

Charles T. Harvey making a test run, December 7, 1867.

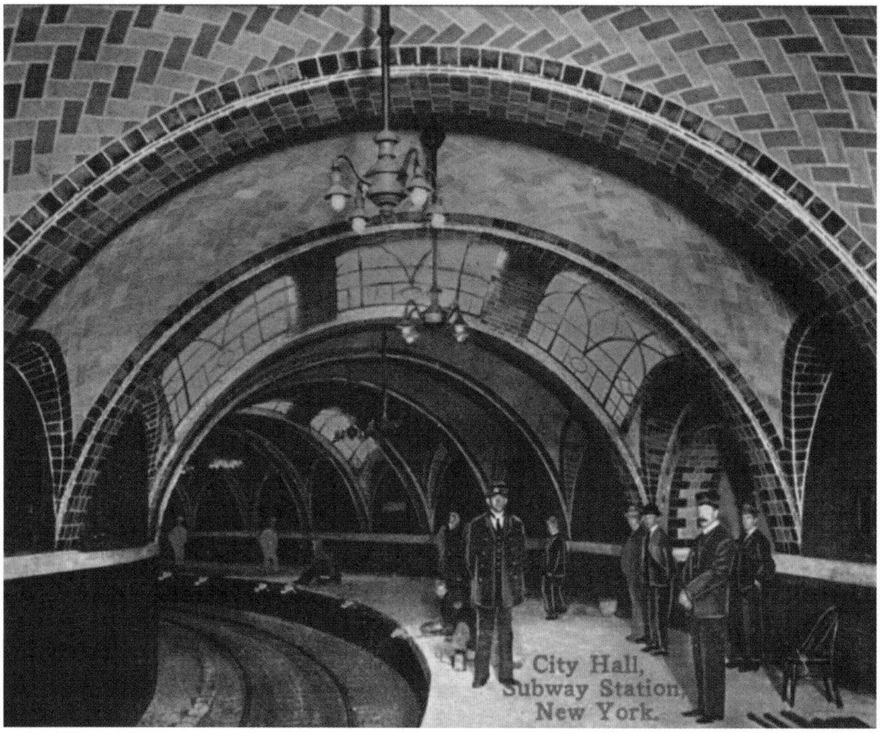
City Hall,
Subway Station,
New York.

The now-abandoned City Hall station, which was the focus of the 1904 subway opening ceremonies.

Even though elevated train lines were becoming quite prevalent in the city, interest grew for developing an underground rapid transit railroad, partly in competition with other cities and partly to help develop outlying areas. Construction of these early subways was grueling. Building crews had to excavate the subway lines by hand. This was slow, difficult, and dangerous work. The New York City subway tunnels required close to eight thousand laborers. Thousands were injured during construction, and some died.

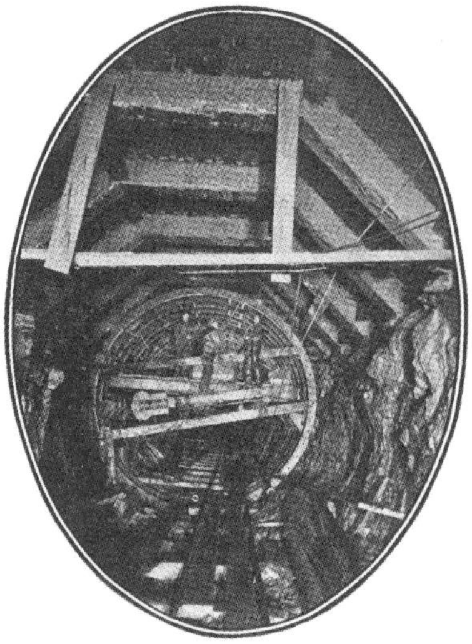

Rock work at the entrance to the East River Tunnel.

The first underground line was opened on October 27, 1904, almost thirty-five years after the first elevated line (and in the same part of town)! When the system opened for business, more than one hundred thousand people stood in line to take a ride on the first subway train. The new system featured many innovations, including the use of electric power, which helped reduce the city's air pollution. Also unique was the four-track design that could run at both local and express speeds. At the time, it was the fastest public transportation system in the world. Hence the slogan: "City Hall to Harlem in 15 minutes!"

H. M. Pettit, Illustrations from January 31, 1903, Harpers Weekly.

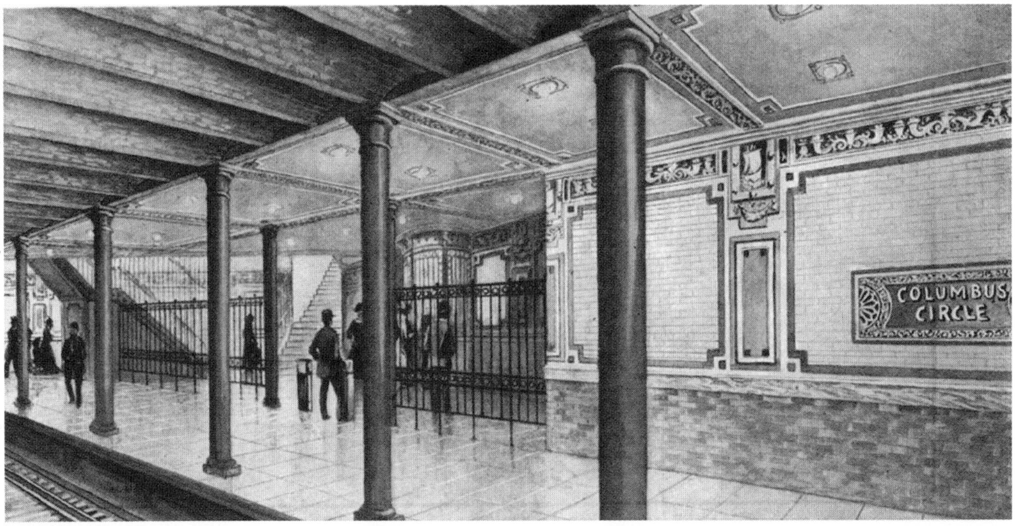
COLUMBUS
CIRCLE

A 1903 illustration of the proposed subway station at Columbus Circle, showing architectural details.

Arthur Weindorf, Architectural Rendering, 1935, Avery Architecture and Fine Arts Library.

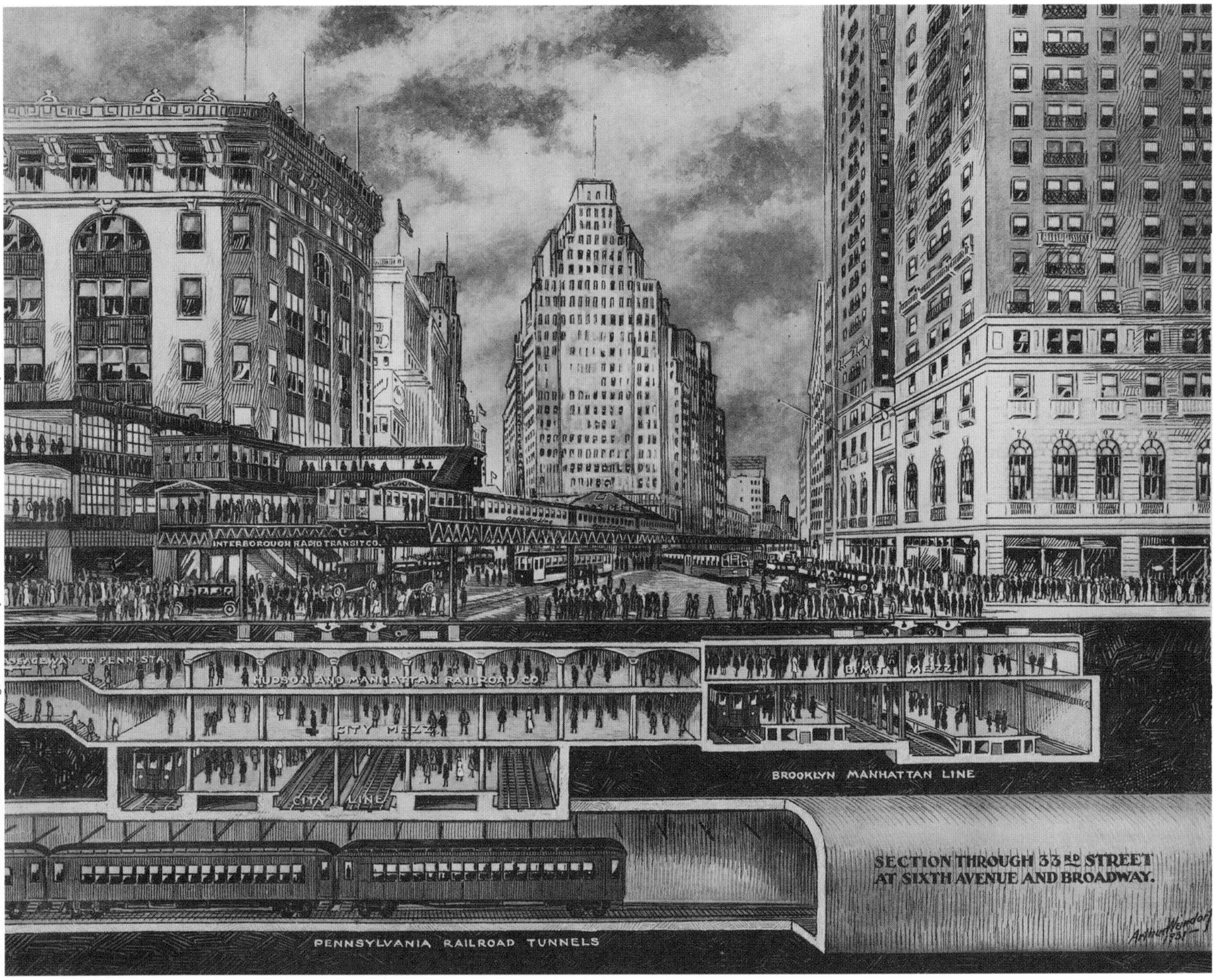
INTERBOROUGH RAPID TRANSIT CO.
PASSAGEWAY TO PENN. STA.
HUDSON AND MANHATTAN RAILROAD CO.
CITY MEZZ.
CITY LINE
B.M.T. MEZZ.
BROOKLYN MANHATTAN LINE
SECTION THROUGH 33RD STREET
AT SIXTH AVENUE AND BROADWAY.
PENNSYLVANIA RAILROAD TUNNELS

A 1935 cross-section view of the underground and elevated transportation network at 34th Street and 6th Avenue (Herald Square). The building on the left is Macy's Department Store.

COMPETING TRANSIT COMPANIES

In the beginning, the subway system was built by two separate private companies, the IRT (Interborough Rapid Transit) and the BMT (Brooklyn-Manhattan Transit). This created two different networks of trains, which did not connect to each other. The IRT and the BMT were hit hard during the Great Depression in the 1930s. On June 1, 1940, the city took over the companies and began a slow unification of the system. It closed many of the elevated lines and created new transfer tunnels to connect the two networks.

West

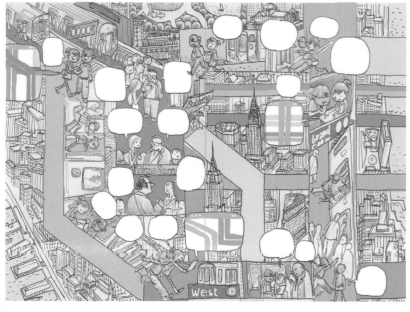

Although now unified into a single network, there are still traces of the competing companies in the subway today. The numbered train lines were part of the IRT system. The J, L, M, N, Q, R, and Z were part of the BMT. The A, B, C, D, E, F, and G were part of a third company run by the city's Board of Transportation itself, called the IND (Independent Subway System). The trains on the letter lines (BMT/IND) are longer and wider than those on the number lines (IRT). Therefore, an A train cannot fit into a 6 train tunnel.

EUCLID AVE
EUCLID AVE
A

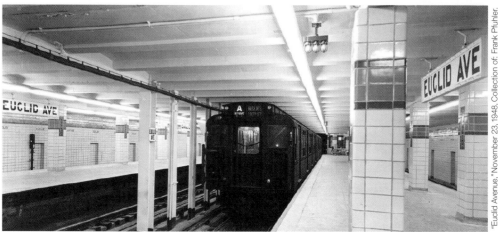

Brand new station at Euclid Avenue on the IND Fulton Street Line (A, C), just before service began running on the line, November 23, 1948.

"Euclid Avenue," November 23, 1948, Collection of: Frank Pfuhler.

WHY ARE THERE NO H, I, K, O, P, T, U, V, W, X, OR Y TRAINS?

The H, K, T, V, and W trains did once exist, but they have since been closed or combined with other subway lines. These letters get recycled as new trains are created. For example, when the new 2nd Avenue train line opens, it will be called the T train. I and O were skipped because they looked too much like 1 and 0. Y and U were skipped because they sound too much like "why" and "you," and the MTA was afraid people would get confused. X is used as a placeholder by the MTA when it is planning new subway lines and so can never be a real train. That leaves only the P train. P trains have been planned in the past but have been abandoned or renamed at the last minute. There's no proof, but it's possible that the MTA simply thinks a P train would cause far too many giggles.

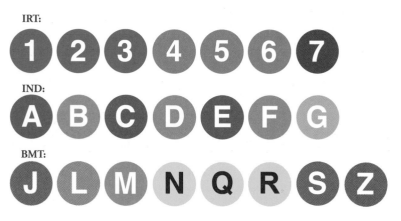

IRT:

1 2 3 4 5 6 7

IND:

A B C D E F G

BMT:

J L M N Q R S Z

THE SUBWAY TODAY

Today, the New York City subway system is still digging new lines! One of the most highly anticipated projects is the completion of the 2nd Avenue line, which has been in the works since the 1920s.

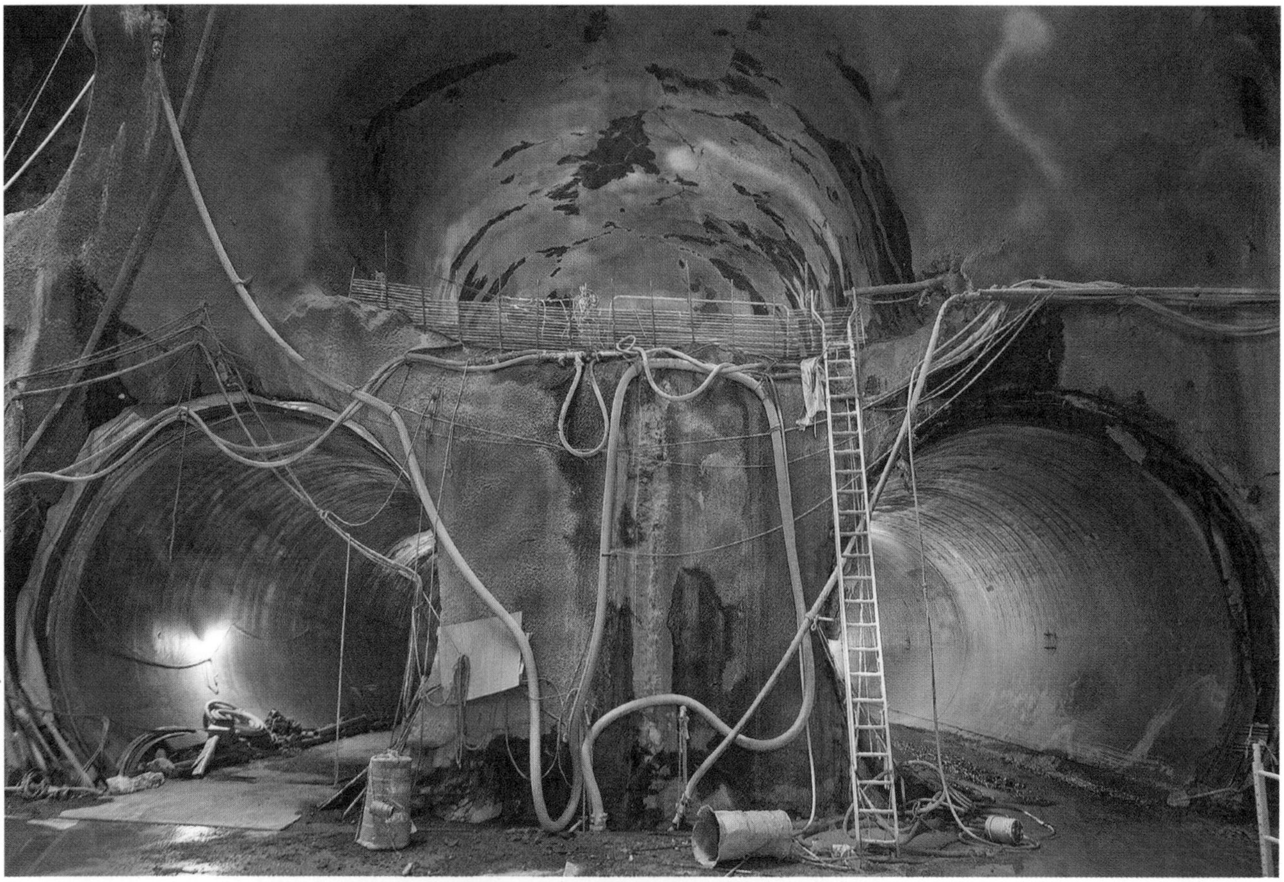

Progress on the 2nd Avenue Subway as of November 23, 2013. This photo shows the future 86th Street Station.

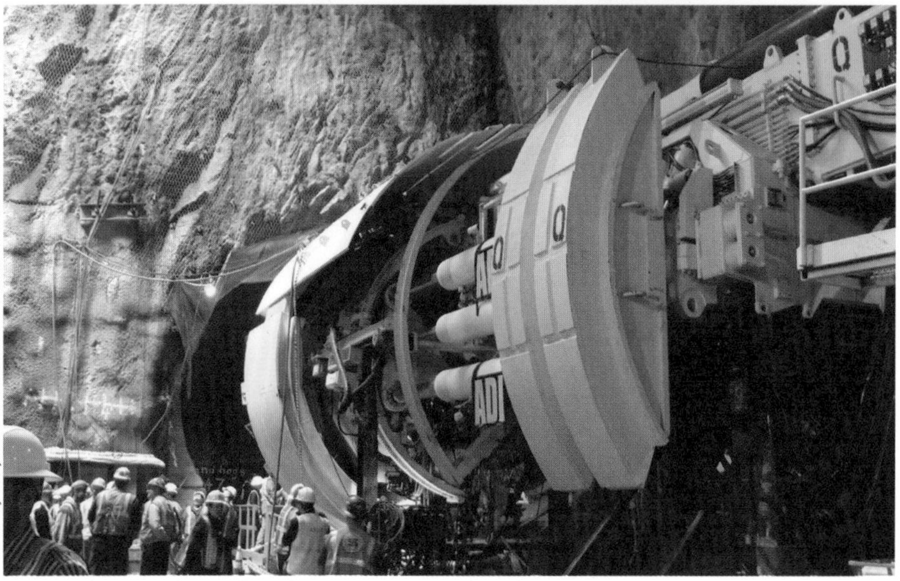

Tunnel-boring machine in the 2nd Avenue subway, May 14, 2010.

These days, a tunnel-boring machine (TBM) does most of the difficult digging. With powerful discs and scrapers, a TBM crushes and removes rock debris in both bedrock and soft soil. It also uses many supports to safely hold up the tunnel as it moves. The only downside is that it moves very slowly, averaging a speed of thirty-five feet per day.

EMPIRE STATE BUILDING

At 1,250 feet, the Empire State Building was the world's tallest skyscraper for over forty years, until the construction of the World Trade Center in 1972. It is now the second tallest building in New York City after One World Trade Center, which reaches 1,776 feet.

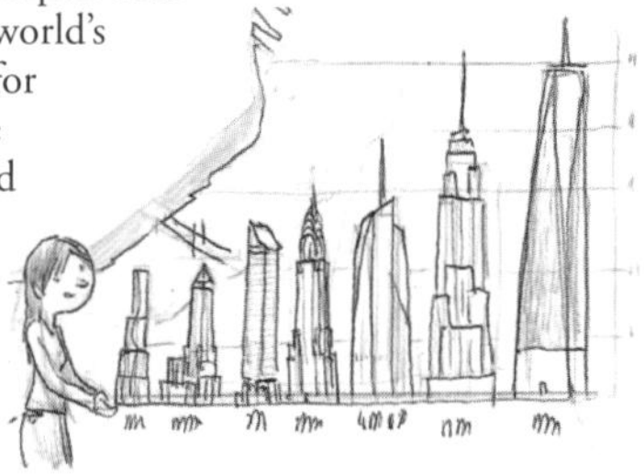

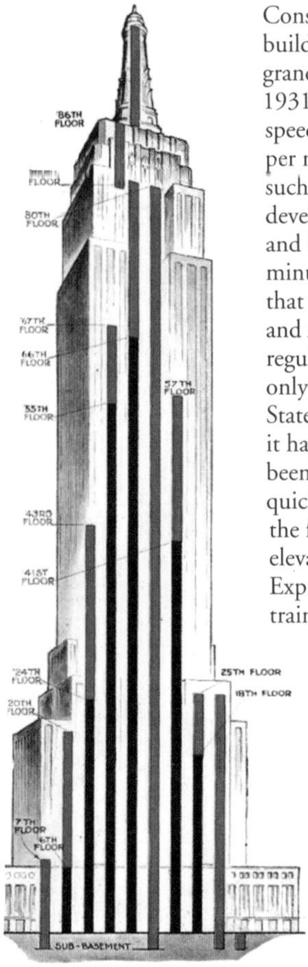
86TH FLOOR
80TH FLOOR
43RD FLOOR
41ST FLOOR
24TH FLOOR
20TH FLOOR
25TH FLOOR
18TH FLOOR
7TH FLOOR
SUB-BASEMENT

Construction on the Empire State building began in 1930, and the grand opening was held on May 1, 1931. At the time, there was a speed limit for elevators: 700 feet per minute. This was too slow for such a tall skyscraper, however, so developers took a bit of a gamble and installed 1,200-foot-per-minute elevators. They expected that the Board of Standards and Appeals would amend the regulations on elevator speed, and only six months after the Empire State Building opened in 1931, it happened. The cars, which had been traveling at the lower speed, quickly sped up, creating one of the first fully functional express elevator systems in New York City! Express elevators, like express trains in the subway, skip certain stops to move thousands of people a day to the upper floors more quickly.

From "Robot Elevators to Serve 85,000 in Greatest Building" (Popular Science Monthly, 1931). Express elevators are marked in black; local elevators are marked in red.

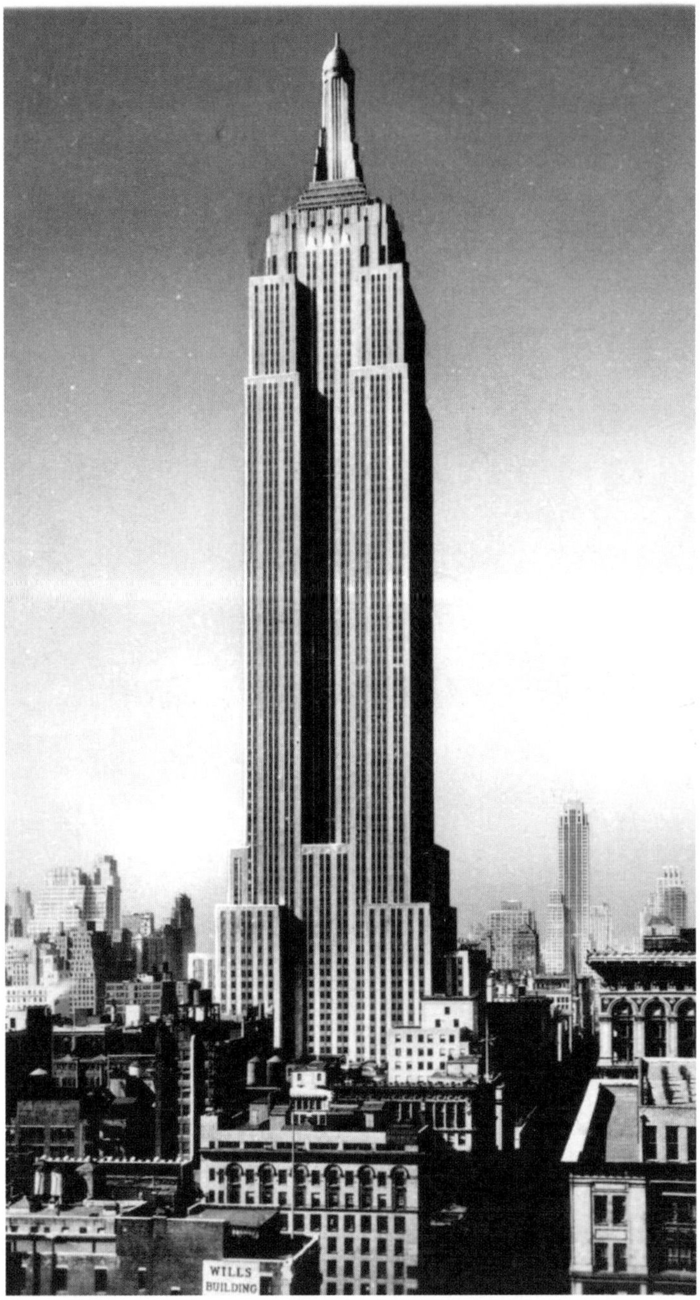
WILLS BUILDING

1948 tourist postcard for the Empire State Building.

FURTHER READING & RESOURCES.

The history of New York City and the New York City Subway System is complex and fascinating. Here's a list of books and websites you might enjoy:

THE CITY BENEATH US: BUILDING THE NEW YORK SUBWAY; New York Transit Authority with Vivian Heller. W.W. Norton, 2004. *Official history of the subway system, with photographs. Ages 10+*

SUBWAYS: THE TRACKS THAT BUILT NEW YORK CITY; Lorraine B. Diehl. Clarkson Potter, 2004. *An easy to read, informative history of the New York Subway system. Ages 12+*

THE SUBWAY AND THE CITY: CELEBRATING A CENTURY; Stan Fischler with John Henderson. Frank Merriwell, 2004. *A big book with lots of history and lots of pictures. Ages 14+*

NEW YORK UNDERGROUND: THE ANATOMY OF A CITY; Julia Solis. Routledge, 2004. *An exciting overview of the tunnels, trains, mazes and secrets underneath New York City. Ages 12+*

THE HISTORICAL ATLAS OF NEW YORK CITY: A VISUAL CELEBRATION OF 400 YEARS OF NEW YORK CITY'S HISTORY; Eric Homberger. Owl Books, 2005. *A comprehensive reference book containing maps, photos, and drawings. Ages 12+*

Online Resources:

WWW.MTA.INFO *The official website of the Metropolitan Transportation Authority, which oversees the subways, trains, and buses of New York City.*

WWW.NYCSUBWAY.ORG *A website dedicated to the history of the subway system, including photos, maps, and documents.*

Tips for Parents, Teachers, and Librarians:
TOON GRAPHICS FOR VISUAL READERS

TOON Graphics are comics and visual narratives that bring the text to life in a way that captures young readers' imaginations and makes them want to read on—and read more. When the authors are also artists, they can convey their creative vision with pictures as well as words. They can enhance the overarching theme and present important details that are absorbed by the reader along with the text. Young readers also develop their aesthetic sense when they experience the relationship of text to picture in all its communicative power.

Reading TOON Graphics is a pleasure for all. Beginners and seasoned readers alike will sharpen both their literal and inferential reading skills.

Let the pictures tell the story

The very economy of comic books necessitates the use of a reader's imaginative powers. In comics, the images often imply rather than tell outright. Readers must learn to make connections between events to complete the narrative, helping them build their ability to visualize and to make "mental maps."

A comic book also gives readers a great deal of visual context that can be used to investigate the thinking behind the characters' choices.

Pay attention to the artist's choices

Look carefully at the artwork: it offers a subtext that at first is sensed only on a subliminal level by the reader and encourages rereading. It creates a sense of continuity for the action, and it can tell you about the art, architecture, and clothing of a specific time period. It may present the atmosphere, landscape, and flora and fauna of another time or of another part of the world. TOON Graphics can also present multiple points of view and simultaneous events in a manner not permitted by linear written narration. Facial expressions and body language reveal subtle aspects of characters' personalities beyond what can be expressed by words.

Read and reread!

Readers can compare comic book artists' styles and evaluate how different authors get their point across in different ways. In investigating the author's choices, a young reader begins to gain a sense of how all literary and art forms can be used to convey the author's central ideas.

The world of TOON Graphics and of comic book art is rich and varied. Making meaning out of reading with the aid of visuals may be the best way to become a lifelong reader, one who knows how to read for pleasure and for information—a reader who *loves* to read.

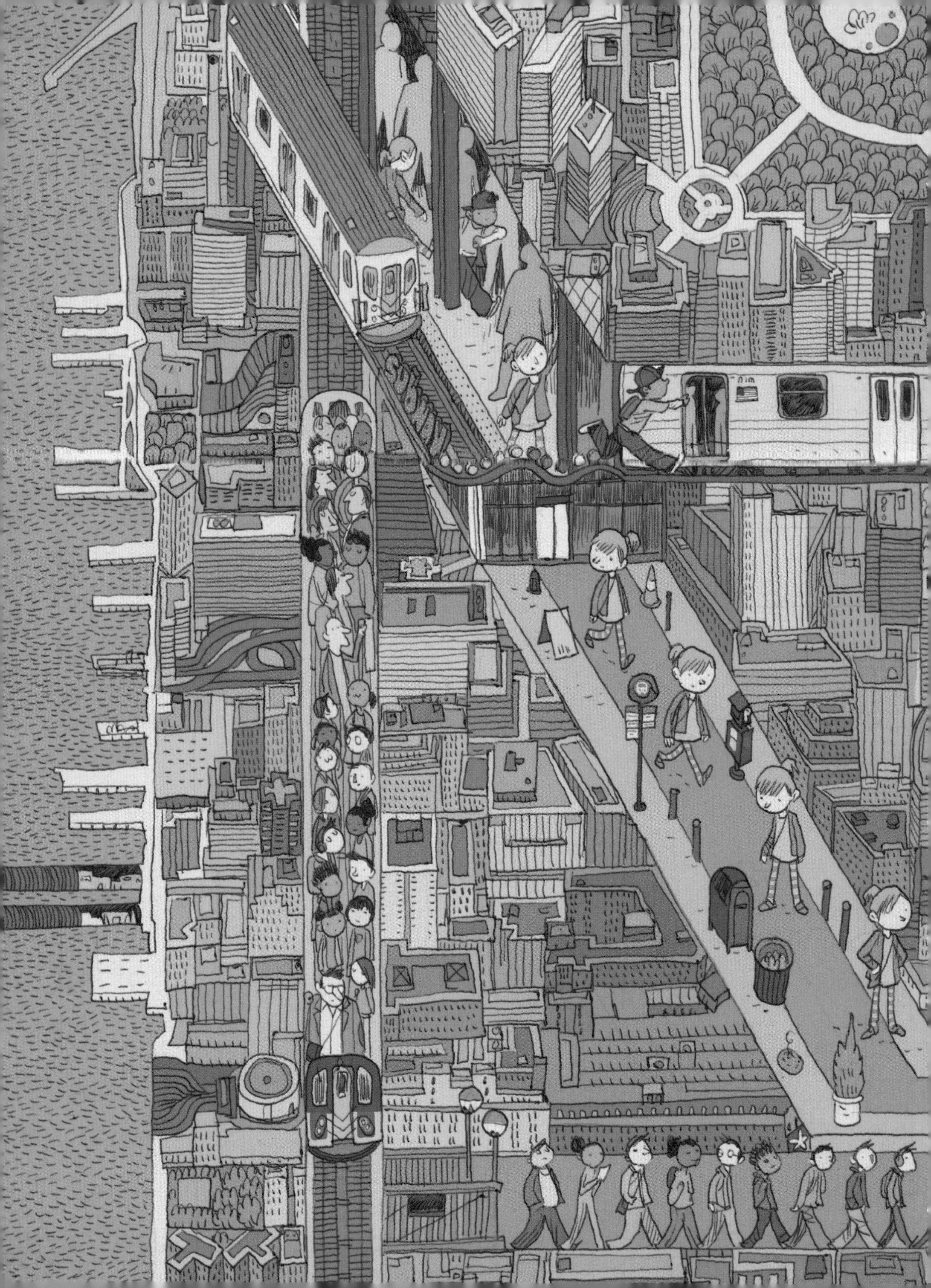